NE

Irving Feldman was born in Coney Is...
attended City College of New York ...
has taught at the University of Puerto ... College, and
the University of Lyon in France. His poems have appeared in *The
New Yorker, Harper's, The Atlantic Monthly, The American Review, Par-
tisan Review,* and other magazines, and his collections of poems to
date include *Works and Days, The Pripet Marshes* (nominated for the
National Book Award), *Magic Papers, Lost Originals,* and *Leaping Clear*
(also nominated for the National Book Award). Mr. Feldman has
earned numerous awards and grants, including a Guggenheim Fel-
lowship and the National Institute of Arts and Letters Award. He is
married to the sculptor Carmen Alvarez Feldman and is a professor of
English at the State University of New York at Buffalo.

NEW AND
SELECTED POEMS

IRVING FELDMAN

PENGUIN BOOKS

Penguin Books Ltd, Harmondsworth,
Middlesex, England
Penguin Books, 625 Madison Avenue,
New York, New York 10022, U.S.A.
Penguin Books Australia Ltd, Ringwood,
Victoria, Australia
Penguin Books Canada Limited, 2801 John Street,
Markham, Ontario, Canada L3R 1B4
Penguin Books (N.Z.) Ltd, 182–190 Wairau Road,
Auckland 10, New Zealand

First published in the United States of America in simultaneous hardcover and
paperback editions by The Viking Press and Penguin Books 1979

Library of Congress Cataloging in Publication Data
Feldman, Irving, 1928–
New and selected poems.
I. Title.
PS3511.E23N4 1979b   811'.5'4   79-14330
ISBN 0 14 042.269 2

Printed in the United States of America by
American Book–Stratford Press, Inc., Saddle Brook, New Jersey
Set in VIP Garamond

All these poems originally appeared in the following periodicals in somewhat different
form: *American Poetry Review, The American Review, The Atlantic Monthly, Bellevue Press,
Boundary 2, Carleton Miscellany, Columbia University Forum, Commentary, Harper's,
Harper's Bazaar, Kenyon Review, Literary Review, Michigan Quarterly Review, Midstream,
New American Review, New Leader, New Mexico Quarterly, New World Writing, The New
York Times, The New Yorker, Poetry, Present Tense, Prism, Saturday Review, TriQuarterly,
Virginia Quarterly Review, Yale Review.*

Para CARMEN y FERNANDO

AUTHOR'S NOTE

Many of these poems differ in small ways from their last printed versions.

CONTENTS

From WORKS AND DAYS

(1961)

THE SAINT

God, you were the handle to every door
And I walked the world unlocking them
To find only myself. I see the poor
And starve, the naked are my shame,
The evil undo, the sick burn
Me, the wretched are my sorrow.
I never wanted this—so to be torn
By the plow of pity in every furrow.

I wanted only to be there,
And be still and slowly to grow
Empty and round, be all in my ear
And listen for your endless Now.

But goodness gives me away from you,
For love has scattered my soul through
Fields and towns. I rise like grass
Against myself, so thick I cannot pass
To you till I wither in every part.
God, I would have been your hollow gulf!
Why did you put your dam across my heart
To overwhelm me with myself!

THE PROPHET

I am your stone. I seek the center.
Lean back, bend over, I know one way.
You cannot move. I weigh. I weigh.
I am your doom. Your city shall not burn.
The flood has gone by, the fever passed.
Get home. Empty the square
As your hearts are empty. Only I am there.
Everywhere. I bring all things down.

Your eyes wander to the ground.
You yearn for density, the solid,
You want blocks, you want the hardest matter:
Clay will not do; granite, not marble.
Your souls crave no room. All is brought together.
You shall be as stone and wedge yourselves down.
Where all things are one.

FLOOD

To Lionel Trilling

The first day it rained we were glad.
How could we know? The heavy air
Had lain about us like a scarf, though work
Got done. Everything seemed easier.
In the streets a little mud.

With the first faint drops, a tiny breeze
Trembled the corn silk, and the frailest leaves
Turned on their stems this way and that.
Coming from the fields for lunch
I thought it my sweat.

4

On the second day streamlets ran
In the furrows; the plow stuck,
The oxen balked. On the third day
The rain ran from the roof like a sea.
I thought I would visit town.

Farmers from their farms, merchants from stores,
Laborers, we filled the town. I
Stayed with a cousin. We were told
The granary was full, we could live
A thousand days should the river rise impetuously.

The fifth day the clouds seemed hung
From the tops of the tallest trees. The sun
We did not see at all. And the rain
Beat down as if to crush the roof.
I did not shave or write my wife.

On the sixth day, we moved the women
And children to the town church, built
On the highest ground hard by the granary.
We finished work on the levee.
The river was thick with silt.

A dark drizzle started in my head.
Next day it trickled on the walls of my skull
Like black earth drifting down a grave.
We resolved to stay in the church come what will.
That day I did not leave my bed.

From where the rain? and why on us?
Not even the wisest knows or dares guess.
Did we not plan, care, save, toil,
Did we lie idle or lust, did we waste or spoil?
Therefore, why on us?

The husbandman from his flock,
Husband from wife, the miser from his heap,
The wise man from his wit, from her urn

The widow—tumbled, as a man might knock
The ashes from his pipe.

And the days descended in a stream,
So fast they could not be told apart.
In the church all went black.
Once I lay with Lenah as in a dream.
Another time I found myself at Adah's back.

If no one gets up at dawn to wind
The clock, shall not the state run down?
If no one gets up to go to the fields
To feed the cows, to sow the wheat,
To reap, how shall the state grow fat?

One comes telling us Noah has built a boat
That through the flood he may ride about,
And filled it all with animals.
Just like the drunk, the fool, that slut-
Chaser, to think of no one else.

I feed my friends and kin; twenty-nine thrived
In my home. But mad Noah harangues the air
Or goes muttering in his cuff
As though a god were up his sleeve.
Who is Noah to get saved?

I am a farmer, I love my wife,
My sons are many and strong, my land is green.
This is my cousin, he lives in town,
An honest man, he rises at dawn.
We were children together.

Shall not the world run down?
Why on us? Did we not plan?
Does not black blood flow before my eyes
And blackness brim inside my skull?
Did we lie idle? Did we spoil?

6

Out of its harness the mind wild as a horse
Roams the rooms and streets. There are some that say
Noah sits amid the rude beasts in his ark
And they feed one upon the other in the dark
And in the dark they mate. And some say worse:

That a griffin was born, and centaur
And sphinx hammer at the door.
Groans and moans are heard, by some the roar
Of giant Hippogriff. Still others cry
That all about the earth is dry!

Dry as if no rain had fallen,
As if we were not awaiting the swollen
River, as if the clouds did not sit
On our chimneys, or the waters
Tumble past our windows in spate.

And some here say a dove has come,
Sure, they think, the sign of a god.
And others say that Noah walks the street
Puffed with news. But bid him wait!
We are busy with our flood.

THE DEATH OF VITELLOZZO VITELLI

Vitelli* rides west toward Fano, the morning sun
Has spread his shadow before him, his head is cast
Along the road beyond his horse, and now in vain

He works his spurs and whip. For all his speed, his past
Like a heavy wind has thrown his death far before
Him, and not till midday shall he fill the waste

*Murdered by Cesare Borgia in 1502.

Of light he has made with the goldness of his spur
And the greenness of his cape. Then he will stand
At last by the bridge at Fano and know no more

His way than the farmer at noon who looks from his land
To his heart and can't think where next to turn his plow;
Or lovers who have stayed abed and reach a hand

And yet have turned away, even as they do so,
To move their legs and sigh, wearied of their embrace
—Yet nothing else seems worth their while. His road will go

Before him, breaking itself in two ways:
One goes to Borgia in Fano, one toward Rome.
And his shadow rushes upward to his face.

CATO DYING

To Bill Sinz

Indifferent, in this torchlit dark, the restless noise . . .
Of sentries' sharp call, servants' tread,
His son's voice, sinking; they cannot cross
The room to him, nothing can exceed
This space. And so had it been his life long.
Not Cato had he made, but emptiness
He had carved about him. The world was wrong,
And only in this silence was there peace.

Dimly he lifts his head and leaning forward
Sees on the couch his body going away.
Would it leave, when now at last his sword
Gives Cato to himself? Stay, stay!
Circumstance gropes everywhere, and flits

Over the world kindling its harsh whisper.
See where the torch, guttering, impatiently sits
With round arms folding darkness in its fire!

A door is opened from their dark room to his.
Did his friends hear? They would come close, and yet
Are trammeled in the torch; their faces are blood-rose
And crossed by shadows which, like whispers, net.
He throws the petaled sword among the rose-heads,
Disdainfully: even here the world was not
Good. The whispers still, the roses have fled,
With his hands he turns himself inside out.

This joyous space he feels is everywhere,
And yet a point within his chest, and yet beyond
These friends, beyond even the Caesar who hurries here;
So great it is they cannot comprehend.
And he alone knows that Cato is no more:
For nothing now is not the space that Cato is.
The torch is turning petals into rose,
And long, long its tongues speak in his ear.

NON-BEING

And all about him rock—with heavy greyness as of a sigh.
And yet Prometheus saw at once the sardonic humor of the
    place,
How the mountains tilted back their heads against the sky
And twisted out a smile; some such thing passed on his
    face.

After a thousand years he thought he saw the joke,
And began, almost nostalgically, to giggle; even his joints
Felt a certain lightness, it took so little to provoke
A knee, merely, say, the wryness of two opposing points.

Another aeon passed and he laughed outright;
He felt himself, in fact, the universal satirist,

The final glittering of the rictus of cosmic spite.
Then nothing really mattered—and his mirth bubbled off in a
    mist.

What terrible cackle bounds blatant through the vale?
O come to the mountain and see a suit of clothes on a nail!

THE OLD MEN

Ho! Persephone brings flowers, to them
new styles in spring. In seven glittering
greys, under round grey hats of straw
—lo! to the fifing sun's tune
the old men come on, stride, march,
drill, straight as the ties of lovers!
(And their bones have drawn together
in gentle communities of joints,
like weary soldiers dreaming head to head.)

Hup, they go, ho! in grey jackets,
grey shoes, sleek as boys, smiling,
striding on, the gay granite legions,
Persephone's grooms, all together, raise
chins, link arms, step out, hiking, marching,
down down into the earth!

WORKS AND DAYS

To my son Fernando

My name is Laughter, and I laughed
Knowing everything's absurd.
For God in his ironic craft
Made all more and less than his word.

And the world dances on the spit
Of my tongue—whirling, leaping, crying
Delight within my fiery wit!
And I laugh all the while I am dying.

THE ARK

Ghetto-born, depression-bred,
Squeezed between the finger and thumb
Of Famine and traditional Dread,
I learned all history's a pogrom.

Scared tutelage of the dead.
The hand that strokes the silken shawl,
I learned, may not strike red.
A Jew's defense, the Wailing Wall.

Learned to be patient under blows,
Suspect the world, yet ready to be
Wiped across my neighbor's nose,
Chided then for being filthy.

Learned the cost of life in cents,
To measure every ring and rag.
Saw Israel's shining tents
Fold up like a doctor's bag.

Learned the little-bourgeois ruse;
To save the day against the night,
And night for day, then lose
Them both, worrying if I was right.

Free of the flood, our ghetto tied
Smugly to the rope of His wrath,
We thought to put the world aside
Like the dirty ring after a bath.

◆

The fog in curtains under the lamps,
Kitchen vapors on the pane,

Smoke puffing out with cramps,
Distant gossip in the drain.

Furniture that I recall:
Solemn lumbar embassy,
Plump and bowing from the wall
To whisper, Comfort's ecstasy.

Sleep! those lotus-eaters said,
A conspiracy in the bowels restores
The interlocking trust of bread.
Sleep alone never bores.

A liver lounging in a pot;
Mama boiling the kitchen runes.
Always I see her face a blot
In the sacred oval of the spoons.

Grey and sweet and shining eyes,
Freckled arms that took with ardor
The scalds and bundles of sacrifice
—To fill and fill again love's larder.

She kneeled to dust the furniture,
But rose with an abstracted eye.
What was it she had seen there?
In spite of all, people die.

In spite of every daily care,
The wash, the rent, sickness, meals,
The building of a life is air,
For death is something else.

The pot grew cool by afternoon
And wore a smiling beard of tears.
A drop crawled drowsily down,
And fell, like the falling years.

The radiator knocked like a ghost,
Outside, the wind and bawling cats.

My father nodded at his post,
Messiah thundered fireside chats.

Papa—shy, sour, slow—
Enduring the worried years like a stone,
Falling, falling asleep over the radio,
Dreaming of his son.

That all proclaimed the quotidian,
And should the day ache with glory,
Prescribed a little medicine.
Grandeurs of our infirmity.

Fed up with the narrow pot,
Every day I ate disgust.
Dishes, death, closet of rot,
Who invented the can of dust!

Well, I flew away from all that—
The old rock, the old ark
Hung aloft on Ararat—
Crow lost in a world of wrack.

WRACK

A lonely music rose and bid
Me follow. And I went.
Under the night's unwaking lid
I learned what dying meant.

And dressed myself in mourner's weed
And ashes of a fallen son,
Thinking Ishmael's desert seed
Happier than my own,

And being choked with memory
I might thereby blot out my name,
Thought breath came best in beggary.
Hell, it was all the same.

With orphan girls I slept it off,
My patrimony of dust.
Hammered down the nights like a cough:
Ghetto contempt, ghetto distrust.

Wintered, paltry, threadbare things,
I took their nakedness to wrap
My fatted calf—Isaac of strings
And straw, curtains of blue burlap.

Oh, those tenement pastorals,
Dressed in the rags of love and such,
Shepherding little animals
Who asked for nothing needing too much.

◆

Her sweat, mascara, breasts implied
The wherewithal to float an affair,
And to her poverty testified
A certain lankness, pallor of hair.

At dawn her eyes opened wide,
Like doors on an empty hall, the stair,
The street's cold light—till I was outside,
And doubting I had been there.

◆

Along the street a winter wind
Rattled its elementary war.
Breathless armies arrived and grinned,
Entered their trench by a subway door.
Leaflets from trees proclaimed the end.
And the wind came on as before.

Politics

Tant vaut le métier tant vaut l'homme.
—DIDEROT

Of love we planned the total reign,
Yet could not bear each other's words.

Our mutual and the world's disdain
Were all the glue that held our shards.

Too ambitious to be at ease
And too honorable for lies,
Our talents turning our disease,
We festered with the public flies.

Our avid youthful powers would live
Without the common daily sops.
The world held up its leviathan sieve,
The duller ones got caught in jobs.

As for the rest, our mockery
Betrayed us out of plumb and measure:
Our trade became idiosyncrasy,
Our program was a little pleasure.

And so we built our politics
On air, like Israelites
With straw who could not fashion bricks.
Condemning duties, what good were rights!

Yet what is it Leviathan allots?
—Bureaucracy or violence,
His stomach or his teeth. Poor prophets
Of love, we chose the desert, and Jonah's hollow melon.

Forgetting

What was I at twenty? there
In the city streets, winding frown
Of the twilit beast of stone, where
The bodies of youths were drizzling down.

What was I then? I forget.
The falling mystery of my breath
Stands in eyeless walls of regret.
City, incarnation of death!

I sit amid my mortal rain.
Although like Theseus I fought,
I have become what I have slain.

My lamp is glowing red and grave.
But darkness is a greater thought
And seeks me through the cave.

Melancholy

The wind tore the sky to tatters
Above the stone bridges of the Seine,
That winter day the driven rain
Leaned down in long ladders.

And my eye, suspended between
The promised power, the murdered form,
Beheld the luxury of storm,
The pathos of the sighing scene.

Wind, through shreds of greyness scream
And crack the saucers of the stream!
I could not fall, could not rise.

The thought of death, the wind's sieve,
Gathered all I could not live
And all the rest shook down in cries.

Division

The world is parted where I pursue
The horizon's river in its flight.
And now its sadness like a night
Is darkening the brown, the blue.

Such a line a child might tie
Across the whiteness of a plane,
And then with godly paint ordain:
Let this be earth, let this be sky.

For me, the line I cannot cross.
In exile, mourning I endure
Every dying, every loss.

My eye runs on! my heart clings.
I wait upon the blackened shore,
Remembering the time of kings.

Apocalypse

At the end of Forty-second Street
A broken sun goes down in squalls.
The wind-bewildered twilight
Is blasted on the cracking walls.

The bells begin, against the stone
They butt their swollen volumes of doom,
The auto horns cry out, Atone!—
From their jobs the poor go crowding home.

Ragged glory of the day's
Dying; winter riots on the drum,
Summoning the poor to their patience.
Salvation is a growing numb.

The bells are pounding the last glint.
Where Seventh Avenue makes a cross,
Grazing on the shores of print,
They await the coming bus.

◆

Slowly the boards rot and leach
Away in the subtle storm of time.
In the soughing, cords begin their screech,
Nails are rusted under the rime.

The will then lashes itself to the helm,
But the rudder jams and wheel fails.
The mast no longer holds its realm,
And now the lungs float out like sails.

And all is slow, still, and grave,
The cargo turned a sandy waste.
And what seemed once the dashing wave
Is but the shiftings of your dust.

◆

But tell me, how else, what else, shall
A prodigal crow fly out to see?
Being no more than a prodigal
Miser prodigal of misery.

Though foreign then, I kept the faith,
Pious still in the old ways;
Guided through the years by the wraith
Of chickens all those Fridays.

The ghost began to trouble my soup.
Among the noodles, smoking breath
Stirred the cowardice in my cup.
Afraid to live, afraid of death.

And so put by the things of man,
All became as one to me—
Packed in the absolute can,
Tinned into Eternity.

The lands I saw, conditions, men,
I thought unworthy of poetry.
Snob of the Absolute, in my pen
Blood turned the ink of mockery.

Death and myself were all I saw;
Between us desert and wrack spread far.
Beginning bad, the end a flaw:
A foolish thought, *mauvaise histoire*.

And then I saw the ark adrift
Under a sodden sky. I grinned
And thought, Return. Like a handkerchief
Its sail stood diapering the wind.

RETURN

Lullaby

For you alone under the eaves
At nightfall I sing these few black notes,
Which then become a sky and go like leaves
Under your lids, upon your throats—

For you alone. For you alone
My fretting wings trace in a little night,
The little night where all your years are one
And I am alone but for your light

To which I sing—for you alone.
I have come close again to watch your sleep;
Now that you are old and children of your son,
Slowly toward you my years creep. And I weep,

Under the eaves for you alone.

Arabian Night

This place, these women talking after dinner,
before they rise to bless goodnight, I should
know them, their stories of the past: sorrows,
children, the dead; those very tales, yes!
sisters, mother, aunt, still as they were,
at the white table in the darkening room
—genies of familial memory, who,
convened, becalmed, by nearness and the night,
rub from a boy's tender pride or impudence,
or cousin's guile, or uncles' merriment
—so innocent, so unredeemed!—
a steady, timid spell against the night.

And I who sit like night at the window
and cannot enter except I become a child—
that light has gone, they cannot conjure him,
not for all their burnished hearts' lamp!

In other lands, striving in chains, he builds
but cannot grow; and I have come in his stead.
And here one is, Time's prosaic Sinbad
returned from dull adventures in the years,
ancient changeling, impostor of a life,
—my treasure flotsam, debased, befouled,
I cannot ransom forth the light, or save
this drifted past abandoned on a hill.

Become the porter of my history,
what can I do but toss this black bag down,
share the relics I've got, knock, return,
like any prodigal—holding out
tarnished gifts to strangers: some guilt,
merely sentimental; a little childish loyalty;
a little useless pity.

Crystal

Be still! I have returned and turned to salt.
Is looking back the only guilt? on the city
in chains, the ark burst out like an apple.
And where are the seeds spilt?
The milk is turning, turning sour on the sill
this summer morning. And all is reverent, poised,
and still, idling, as I do, in the faulted crystal
of the light; clear, beyond recall.
The steaming cornmeal, the table, coffee mill,
the carrots sweetly burning, forlorn nail that waits . . .

Kernel of dawn, crystal of light held
to the eye like pale water flowing,
until the eye fills—crystal
where all is poised and still for a moment
before it falls, as in a tear of salt.
Do they await my word to rouse them to the fall?
Or do I cry because they are chained
in my guilt? I who am salt
on the dawn, a chain of wings on the light.
The sleepers yawn. Even their faulted years

seem a thing newborn and chill this morning,
mama dozing with her bluest apron on
dreaming she wears it to a ball,
and papa dreaming of his son . . .

And I of him this crystal morning.
I have come home again. Be still,
I will cry crystals down to salt the wounds of time.
I alone have come back to know
and knock this morning at the door,
yet they are still, as in a tear, as the sun
that fills the pale water, still as my laughter,
dreaming they are whole.

Scratch . . . scratch. I come tapping the stone,
blind remembering, blindly scratching grief
in the stone, wounds on the tomb of light.
Tap tap. And who will let me in? Will
the crystal open, the ground awake, the dreamers rise?
I have scratched a mark this morning. Is there no seed
for its ground but broken timbers, littered stone?
I have brought a straw. Who will teach me to build?

A POET

From earliest age he'd shown himself an adept of decor
And could not be anywhere long but he was onstage
And obtrusively would produce from pockets a window, a
  door,
A table and chair, strike a pose, and say, "This is Rage."
And accompanied this attitude with prelude and postlude,
Or pointed heavenward to certain platonic flats
Awaiting their *entrée*, or seemed to engage a feud
With spirits under the floor, who were, in fact, under his hat.

I think he wanted to convince us our lives are papers
(Or that his was *not*) written over with the same old word
And folded up into gay little party favors
That go *pop!* and tell an ominous fortune if tugged too hard.
(It may be we *are* such minuscule literature.)
Articulate he was, but mistrusted eloquence,
For *that* pretends that something *is* real and, like Nature,
Can crumple one's performer's-smile with easy indifference.

An unpleasant shipwreck; though for this situation,
Too, he had a name somewhere in his everpresent valise.
For everything, he felt, was named already in the lexicon
Of public dreams—awkward, sad, and noble like his
    properties.
O perhaps he'd been a desolate child who'd murdered by fact,
Named his toys and thought them dead because respondent to
    his strings.
No matter, for now he could be seen at the end of his act
Grinning, grabbing up the tray, and scampering into the
    wings.

Well, and if he liked to pretend, at times, that the wind
He'd invoke to mow down a house of cards was *not* from his
    deck
And had not also, like all his gods, been machined,
Every magician believes that Chaos is the finest trick.
In his Master File of Forms, Norms, and Storms, he sought
    Repose.
But nameless death came and blew them all into a weather,
Deceived, deny it who will, by his Apocalypse-Pose.
It is to be doubted we live as well or die better.

SUMMER GAME

Higher into the half-light,
—While the children flow out
Of their shadows and the twilight

And, soaring and sinking, shout
To follow upward what they have sailed
Higher and slowly turning about—

The great ball their breaths have swelled,
Purging desire with delight,
Is, like the whole soul healed,

There on the summit of flight
Afloat, with no outline to break
It from the sky's descending light,

It also descending, to overtake
You in silhouette by the goal
You haunt and may not forsake,

While, over every bound, the ball
Grows downward from its height,
And sublime, continuous, and sole,

Enormous with all the suffusing light,
Is here. Throw wide your arms,
You! Embrace this world of light!

GOYA

MAN

The soldiers bear a sack,
A white sack without a tear;
The soldiers are in black.
For the rest, the plain is bare.
And what else *should* be there?

They carry the sack,
They do the best they can;

One in his arms, other on his back.
Are these animals? their bag of bran?
No. They are men. This is a man.

"SE APROVECHAN"

"They take advantage"—the soldiers need clothes,
While corpses don't, who have their repose
And nakedness like a second birth,
And nose-down sniff new science from the earth.
So what if nakedness admits the crows!

Such handsome athletic figures,
Twenty centuries of nudes! which now the soldiers
Like bungling apprentices of the muse
Or drunken helpers in a museum cellar,
Yank and tug at to uncover.

And doing so, give that hopeless bric-a-brac
A little of the rhetoric of passion back.
A giant tree with haunches of a mother,
In her anguish torn and flowering and black,
Rears up!—but the head is out of the picture.

OTHER MUTILATIONS: DISASTERS OF THE DEAF

Not sound, no—that's not his—they steal
The silence, their machines have sucked the space
Out through his ears, *his* space, *his* silence, unloosed
The inner volumes of his body; hopeless to feel
Within himself, and in a place.

The eye reposeless; here surfaces crack,
And his eye bewildered, weighted with trying to hear,
Aghast, in the ragged depths, before the huge dim spook
Of skin and stones, the *them!* the horror: the hacked
Cadaver of his space. But right, or left, a path there

Winds away, out of the present, toward a nowhere
Gone, a something or nothing, all white or all black,
Not his or theirs!—but a *path,* escape! like an inward ear.

THE DUELISTS

We look at masker, mask, and think: tree/root,
Face/soul. A pretty word-game wherewith
The world's made one; which these masks refute,
Saying: white/black—surface of no depth,
Depth without surface, as: bare foot/empty boot.

See, the darkness fills an eye or stains
Across a mouth, and their swordpoints daze the air
Like black flies buzzing here/there
That light and leave and touch, as on two windowpanes,
To learn what world of blackness a little mask contains.

THE NIGHTMARES

O Beauty! O . . . but that no longer twists.
Better these after-all harmless succubi
With noses you can grip with both fists,
And dwarfs with humps like a witch's saddle,
Outrageous hairy runts who come knee-high
And No-faces sketched in on a paddle,
And Hot-feet who jump up and down, hop hop,
And cackle and cry and bite their hands, and stop.

Little children, in fact. O may they now come
Unto us, bringing their tantrums of delight;
O, in this banal twilit delirium,
May these idioms, crotchets, slips of the brush
Come daub their mimicries of our human fright.
Well then, is it asking too much
To have, before the frozen night of terrors,
Such charming playmates as these lively errors?

Is it ambition leads him there?
The witty artist starts in air—
Where exclusion, balance, order disclose
An ethereal and delicious pose,
And intimate a phantom doggie and
Imagined feet that stray or stand
Beneath the portrait of a doll.
An art of seeming not to fall.

But hunger brings one back to earth:
To carnival maskers, madmen, clowns,
Dark hordes of cobbleheaded crones,
—The riotous fictions of rebirth—
And odd bones the war has left around;
So much to feed those starving wits,
To be gotten down. But somewhere's a ditch
Of blackness always dropping underground

—To where the monster, lit by a chthonic glow
And having eaten the charming *cogito,*
Now lifts a bloody torso like a toy,
As if, poor thing, there was only one joy;
At the bottom of all, this preposterous end
That wit cannot define or passion comprehend.
And the black holes in the fiercely rounded whites . . .
But be careful! don't touch it!—it bites.

ASSIMILATION

I dreamt the other night I was in Heaven,
That I rose up like a sundae with leaven.
I was there in the Old Folks Home playing pinochle and
    checkers
And up above us is a picture of Old Abe who fried the
    neggers.

Everything is free and Grade A. Then I turn over my card.
It says, "What's good for Ford is good for God."
And all the boys are gathered sitting around the televidge,
Clear as day you can see God's own image.
He talks sweet and low and he looks like Ed Murrow,
The music's by Gilbert and Ed Sullivan; then it all goes
    blurro.
And Maxie whispers, "He's Self-Sponsored, Self-Applauded,
    Self-Rated,
One and Almighty. It's a quality show and never outdated."
"Haha," I say, "boy, that's rich!"
"Shhh," says Bennie, "He owns half of Miami Bich."
But I figure I'll unload 'cause the market looks too bullish.
But Barney whispers, "Don't do nothing fullish!"
So I hang on and buy till the ticker goes screwy
And I'm ten million bucks ahead and the bears are all blooey.
The sky's full of stars going around in their tracks like at
    Graumans Chinese,
And they start handing out autographed menus from Lindys,
The guys're all drunk and there are B-girls and bagels
And free silver dollars straight from Las Vegals
And Bella grabbed me and said, "Hey, we're all angels!"
But I'm worried, why does Mr. Mortie have to run after the
    models?
Can't he stick to his dressmaker's dummy and keep out of the
    Catskills?
That buyer from Phillie! That union contract! O, I wanna
    scream Halp!
Seventh Avenue's waiting for my scalp.
But Gimbels takes a thousand and Macys takes ten and then
    it's bam!
And I buy Rausye a mink for her old persian lamb.
And Grossingers was giving a banquet at Woolwoits
And Sollie was laughing it up trying on the skoits,
And Albie said, "Moishie's under the Boardwalk gettin' laid."
And Sadie said, "Come on, let's go sit in the shade."
And Marvin sank a heaver and Joey hooked from the side,
Then Creepie drove in for a lay-up while the other guys cried.
And Bernie pulled a mousetrap and Skinnie's pass hit the
    mark,

And forever and ever the Mighty Babe stood swattling 'em
    outta the park.
Then after the spelling bee we have a map-drawing contest
Of the United States and teacher says mine's the best.
But Sidney and me, we snuck into the Loews
And this guy sits down and starts tickling our knees.
And I say "Leave us alone, mister," and he says, "Say please."
And then he says, "Wanna see the scar under my kiltie?"
And I look and oh my god it's Uncle Miltie!
And they all think the Lone Ranger is really a crook,
And on the street papa says hello to Mr. Bashook.
Then the kids all pile in and we start throwing rocks.
On the radio Uncle Moe says, "Irving, there's a present in the
    icebox."
God, I feel all soft, I wanna cry and twitch.
There's a card, it says, "For your throat, a thirty-year itch."
And there's a can the size of a man, and mama's in it!
"Mama," I cry, "I found you again!" "Don't talk," says she,
    "itt!"
And I'm standing in my crib and I say, "Papa, buy me a tri-
    cycle."
And he spreads his wings and smiles like the American Ikele.
And it's always dark and everything's free and you never hear
    No.
But I can't breathe and think I'll drown in the stuff and
    nobody'll know.
And I wake up kicking and screaming, "Lemme go! Lemme
    go!"

THE LOST LANGUAGE

I have eaten all my words,
And still I am not satisfied!
Fourteen thousand and twenty blackbirds
Hushed under my side.

And when I think of what I have written
Or might have and can and shall write
—My life, this appetite,
But how shall I eat the food I've forgotten?
And think of how my envy like a lust
Kept me up all night with its tease,
And how the night unveiled a noble bust
When I thought of glory—but that doesn't please.
So much ambition,
And so little nutrition.

Après le déluge, moi.
There it is, all the sad tale—
A perfect postdiluvian male,
And other humanist ta-ran ta-ra.
For, after all, it's only disgrace,
At the very best, to outlive
(Half-monadnock, half-sieve)
The saddest thing in the life of the race.

And when I think how many fathoms deep
Debris of that mighty birth . . .
O then there were words in the earth
That were the things they named
And lay like manna in easy reach,
And when you spoke, there was speech.

Very hungry and not a little ashamed,
For passion is no longer food,
I have taken up again,
In ghostly parody, pot and pen,
And sit to gnaw my chattering brood.

One cup of Lethe and it's always too late.
Where are you, *O liebe brayt?* *

* *Yiddish: O beloved bread.*

From THE PRIPET MARSHES

(1965)

PROLOGUE

I in the foreground, in the background I,
and the stone in the center of all,
I by the stone declaiming, I
writing here, I trundling in
the moody mountain scene, the cardboard
couples, the dusty star, I turning
from the page, my hand staying moonlit,
my pen athwart the light, I dimming
the moon with cloud, the scene then pensive,
uneasy, and seated colossal
on the Earth's round brink I, my head bending
my hand back at the wrist, thinking,
thinking . . . And, still by the stone, I
attent to my declamation, taking it down.

So the mind above its theater, on
restless wing aloof, circles
in a thin ether of pain. And I
the more outside holding the global
thing at arm's length, the sphere withdrawing
its rounded perfection. Night falling
there, I prompt the little towns to wink,
show faces sudden at windows, peering
from the radiant blocks; I transmit
the earnest domestic effulgence to

33

the endless stars, I declare those lives
indispensable, good, and I think, I think. . . .

The stone, too, floats off, swaying its wide
circle, taking the all along. I
bodiless, watching it go, sipping
the transparent pain, the void, sending
my message after it. It goes off,
gathering the starlight to itself.
And does not shrink. I afterward
melancholy, thoughts thinking . . .

THE NURSES

Et vous vous endormez, enfin, dans la blancheur.
—HENRI CALET

Like weary goddesses sick of other worlds—
those little islands, their drugged white beaches
where the surf's unending colonies arrive,
and, helpless, the sacrifice lies on altars
of their indifference, gasping in the sun,
offering millenniums of his wound—

they, as from the prows of ships stepping,
come to where the patient worries
the sheet's spreading day, his body
stilled in drowsy rituals of disaster.
And the marble paradigms, their patient,
uncaring hands, drop from the salt-parched
light, gathering your infinite gift,
its burden.

And they whisper,
My prince, my son, relax, forget, give in.

And your memories crowd away into
the gleaming trough, the incurable loss,
where you dissolve, begin to go off,
receding, curling away like a wave,
no, like a point. And who will hold you now?
—falling asleep in the whiteness without end.

Their voices float after you in other worlds,
other bodies, their hands dwell in your minutest death.

ARTIST AND MODEL

After Picasso's Suite de 180 dessins

THE ABDUCTION

1

Carefully, he set an easel out,
a page (white), which made the site
a cave, thrusting who had been
beside him, she, seized, captured, beyond the plane,
yet not forever into shadow.
On his side, he, O in a motley of loss—chattering
secretive, sad febrile, sick animal,
credulous sly, monkey pensive. And she,
cast away and dormant, lying-in, a model,
sample, sign pointing mysteriously
from the darkness outward to herself,
what she was, is, still to be, beyond the cave.

THE SUBJECTION

2 She

And not less is, cannot be more,
all center, surface, herself,

continuous simulacra rising
outward to this form, what here she is,
offered in the cave, there flying and glinting
on a hill, spume aloft and facet,
and in the forest there on all
the trees at once dazzled like a wind.

3

And does she think? What thought is possible
to that body's absolute curve, head, its
supple repose? Then, if anything,
a rhythm of becomings, herself, her
innermost, most infinitesimal
simulacrum in triumph on waves
of rosiness riding to her skin.
Quickly, this ease he translates
to opportunities, discovers answers,
landfalls, clues to a something hidden
where he has left the leavings of his brush
—in armpits and legpit a splotch,
trickle of hair: three sapient beards.

4   *Monkeyshines*

To his glance opening, teasing
to a gaze nowhere repulsed, never
satisfied, eludes, confuses him,
she, so and thus, grave, serene.
And he is cross, tracking this endless clue
to a secret that doesn't exist: her
inside, her other side. And persists, embarks,
paddling his little cave, sail sighting,
Mozambique, Madagascar, still sail,
searches under a buttock, along a thigh,
near ear, dodging among the points
of view, *Qua qua,* chattering, followed by:
spoor of anecdotes, vestigia, mask-droppings.

5

He has his way, his trade—and this,
his maker, set its thumbprint on him,
mark of its power, swirling the lines
of his face over his smock down the page,
where his profile's squiggle is justified,
stayed, in a few satirical dots.
And she, naked, absolute, posing only
the problem of unity—by which light
he recognizes he is grotesque, perverse,
embarks on his dialectic, hopping
about in festinate fury, seeking
a slur, a total perspective, to create
beyond the work her, her garden
without labor, to repossess that innocence.
Ignorant, she stands. Stymie. On his brow
finger delves furrow, there between
the worn bumps of horn, warts of thought.

6

He will set her to work. She listens, stares,
puts on the masks. Why not? the flesh
accommodates, and welcomes home the wanderer.
All ports are one port; the door opens, the bed's
page blank. Another mask. Again, here
in the cave where she remains to furnish
the world to her keeper's cell, subjects
for the endless busyness of mind and hand.
Smiling a myopic squint of mouth,
taking his peek-a-boo of masks for
the gestures of her inwardness, confessions,
expressions, he lays back her head
for abandon or tilts her elbow for offense.
She, upon request, cradles a breast with her hand,
"Like so?" And he, "Hold it!" commands,
snaps to attention like a thumb.

7

As thought will, his haunts the depths,
groundswell, the crucible of pressure,
where the monstrous shape flashes into
the universe of rhythm. So,
trawls his net of lines, hunting
the sunken old Venus, the model's other,
her brine-beaten vestige. And up it comes,
thumping the cave's keel, enormously
beyond its calyx reaching, sublime,
out of the cave, brilliant, defined,
world that, quicker than fish-petal, fin,
flares piquant in the periscopic eye.

8 *Monkey Art*

The purpose of a line is to create
a transparency, a foreshortening of
the total perspective, that what is not
seen can be imagined there where it veers
around and slopes against the backward
space—of the mind, alas! Imitation
is magic, abuse of her good kindness
that requires man's sinew, man's breath
to bring (strike! sing!), declare her to herself.
Stuffed with possession, her effigy
cramping in the perambulator
of his mind, he strides about,
refines her to ovoids such and such, hatches them
as schemes that telescope down
to mines of babel. He looks through,
yes, he sees it, at last! a navel.
Or is it mountains on the moon?

9 *His Monologue*

Cheap tricks, these scribbles and dots,
data to tick, tickle in mental
IBM: breast, nipples, nose. And these
polarities, parallels, rhymes,

dialectics, symmetries; this "like,"
this "stands for"—scum and froth
of convention, squibble and quibble,
boundaries of the mind,
its dark court where fools (two) (Thesis?
Antithesis?) banter a shuttlecock
across a net and call it phoenix,
cry, *My* phoenix. Only the court endures,
persists beyond the badinage of rebirth.
Ground of the mind! Arbitrary lines!
Under the game reclines, out
of its plane, she, reposing, ungraspable:
foothold, mountain, sky.

10 *He Speaks of Her Accommodations*

What I have sought, passage outward
into the garden, where, terror surrendered,
the soul reverts in a shower of seed
—this she presents, dreaming
salvations, appearances, answering
at cave's mouth, tower window,
vocations of hammer, stylus, string,
and shows, in every pose, her happy accident:
trou: trouvaille, the lucky hole-in-One.

THE RAPE

11

With passage of the voice, the thing evoked
drifts back to itself, silence; unblinking
attention, the note sustained until
it screams, only this can hold it here.
All magic fails, the uneasy metaphor
of lines collapses; and ancient
jackanapes must have her all, his feeble
arms cannot gather her greatness,
receding, seemingly poised somewhere
else seemingly beyond flesh.

But now he will enter, deposit his
inwardness, make her soulful, think,
swell with pathos, crumble
to characters and roles—and daubs
her every, her most minute, apparition
with monkey ink.

12 *After*

And, at the last, only ink is, a sea
of sighs and signs, cave darkness, dark
petroleum pool whose old metamorphoses
come, in slow turmoil, surface
rainbow, surface of fire. Of fire
he thinks, living in a charred moment
after the power, seeking the moment
before it shined. And makes another
line, sign: vestige of the power gone,
pointing a power to come
where she, regnant, entire, toward herself
lightly draws him with powerful repose.

BONES FOR THE TOMB OF *VIDE*

Le meilleur fauxmonnayeur

1

Reader: Leprosy can be
A sort of cosmetology.
Naked bone, the eye its witness,
Yes, indeed, naked man
Is not perhaps, perhaps is
The ultimate in decoration.

Lovely, his glance goes on the glass
Slithering after its remotion
In hymens of self-consciousness.

The terse illustrious skeleton
Shone with such calcium calm
It wanted no art to embalm.

2

Reached, reach, reaching, to reach.
Eye's delighting amorous leech
Fingered the stops of his marrow flute.
Oh for the bliss of a nictitation!
In its swelling embouchure his youth
Was singing, Disincarnation!

Englobed—on the fevered lush floor,
Its fierce grass, its murderous seed,
At the vivid stream, on all fours—
In mind's white paradise, *Vide*,
Inflecting toward his embrace,
Reaches, and drinks a little face.

3

Reader: Also prosthesis
Is a sort of mimesis.
Desire made them, the flesh, the volumes,
The power poised on the flying center.
Ruined, the temple. High columns
Cliché around an empty altar,

Assemble, tremble; manipulation
By crank of iron, clanking brace
Confers facsimiles of consolation
If not gratuities of grace.
Reflected from his rictus-posture,
Vide infers he's feeling pleasure.

4

And otherwise his bones disposes,
After the Grammar of Roles and Poses.

So "If desire flashes and plunges:
With option of tear, leer, or sneer,
Place on one's sternum one's phalanges
To signify 'I am sincere.' "

Though, truly, without desire, or, rather,
Knowing it as something he possessed.
Still, there were the laws of matter,
Motion, gravity, and rest—
It was almost like being in nature,
Before the world had parched to paper.

5

Reader: Was the Mirror,
And Mirror begot the Posture,
And it begot the sterile Now,
Seeing the momentary eye seeing
From the white bewrinkled brow
A brow smoothed to a scruple of being.

And that the stream harried his features,
Broke them to points, flares, divisions,
Convinced him he was many creatures.
Proteus of discrete positions,
The caroling metamorphoses
Halt in his dismal cease.

6

He will not die, neither will he
Destroy, being sterilely
The optimist—of revivisections,
Posterities, new futures,
Pages, paradigms of bones,
Successful gangrenes, clever sutures.

Quite undestroyed, though dead,
Mummied, miraculously slim;
His ghostly banneret of head

Flutters and does not sink or swim.
Flashing, fishing, frothing, fuming, with every breath
The river calls: Assume the power! Fulfill the death!

"PORTRAIT DE FEMME"

After Picasso

1

Somewhere between our nervousness and
our admiration, she sits in her portrait
—*une femme,* with two noses, in a striped blouse,
being poked fun at, feeling doubtless
herself honored by this satirist so famous
no one laughs any more, she, the chosen
one, of flippered arms and perfunctory fingers,
a visage clawed in colors, one heartless
breast a blank circle, on her vase-stem
neck imposed, a brow like Gibraltar's.
Maybe it is Dora Maar—"charming, talented,
vivacious"—composed here on a collapsing
chair between three jokes (on the flesh,
on vanity, on painting)—whose iron mouth
and clear fixated gaze betray to all
the world only the fiercest equanimity.

2   *The One Verity*

Flesh is what, exactly? And the spirit—"witty,
vivacious, provocative"—livening it,
what? Mysteries rendered negotiable by
a sly counterfeiter who's countersigned her Maar,
merely, having, ungently, reinvented her all
—one lady, in one chair—and cashed her in
for the small change of relation, except:

the imagined horizontal connecting to one eye
corner the next. The rest is paint.
Behind the eyes on the goblet-head, defined
by the jest of unkiltered metamorphoses, is:
a liquid just level, precariously still. This
not to spill a life long while providing witty
vivacity with vivacious provocation—this
is perhaps the soul and quite enough
to make dear Psyche weary, bright Eros weep.

3 *Who Is Dora? What Is She?*

Perhaps on such a day as this—but
in France in 1936, before,
that is, the War and other events
now too infinite to list (though
out-of-doors the oak whispers not
and the birds exist much as
they did and will) came and went
like that and like this, all things
that time bore and then dismissed
—before the War perhaps, on such
a day as this, Dora Maar (let us
say "Dora Maar," for who would be
anonymous? and her name was all
she really wore) sat in a chair
in 19 and 36 with a wish fierce
and commonplace to be mysterious,
to survive and to thrive, to be a success
and be good, and be covered
with paint like a kiss,
eternally, in nineteen hundred thirty-six.

LITTLE LULLABY

Dark-time. The little ones like bees
have stolen the light, packed it away
in their healthy mandibles and gone off.
Rest, little soul, of your lithe cunnings,
of your tattling tattoo undressed. They
have taken the daylight in their keeping;
safe in the hive, hidden, it will not chide
you if you are silent. At last, listen:
under the fallow sad song of your neighbor's
life, or the blood waltzing in your ear:
dispossessed, uncharming, enormous
bodies approach; they wish to fulfill you.

POEM AT THIRTY-FIVE

Many smile, but few are happy; my friends,
Their lives hardening about them, are stern
With misery, knowing too well their ends.
—But are these destinies, or mock-destinies,
Or both at once? They will answer as they please.
But a spring day arrives at them like a knife.
And they *want* to break out, but that day, too,
Is so hard—yet bravely (for all are brave)
They press against it (and it hurts, be sure); their might
Is all in that, unbroken where the airs move against
Them; they are drawn down to that point. And here the night
Finds them, harder, testing their strength, tensed.

Despair brutalizes. That is the law. (But
Is there music in that?) My friends, feeling
Their lives hardening, grow harder, less appealing;
Almost the past condoning, almost a pleasure
Finding there they cannot in their harder future,

45

Though they know, as we say, the two go together.
So wise men have said all things return.

(Many smile, but few are happy; my friends,
With misery, knowing too well their ends,
Their lives hardening about them, are stern.)

THE MESSENGERS

To those (only to those?)
who abandon all, yes,
to the great abandoners
unliving their lives,
the ecstatic messengers come
unconscious of their tunics'
heartbreaking expressive fall,
their gusty disheveled curls,
their cheeks puffing as if
one second more they will
lift their trumpets and call.

Radiant, they, and always
earliest arriving
to precede the lavish day
like the light prophesying
at dawn, lighting nothing
for nothing yet is born,
they are almost turning
to go, almost are gone,
already spoken the word
delightfully their faces shine,
and fullness of the day
in a blaze of trumpet metal:

See how I love my life!
Faithless,
you have loved your lives too little.

THE DOUBLE

On other cloudy afternoons
you will be sitting here, or pacing
the rooms, your restless words
unuttered. I put you there now
so the drama may continue, with poplars
invoking the wind outside, the lamplight
slowly focusing to a pencil point.
Here, it is murdering an angel
in the very center of everywhere. This same
joy shall be yours, drawing the blood out
among these mazes that continue
always, under the aspects
of a cloudy day.
                    Mysterious the mazes
of those afternoons through which
the red leaves sweep, your own hand
tracing joyfully there another life
to live you on afternoons like this.

CLOWN AND DESTINY

And you improvise; yet there is always
the dead one among the shifting figures,
the old knight in armor fallen on
the stifled ground. And still you continue:
being dog, or starlight, or turning ocean,
yet return always to the one figure
lying hinted among the silences
(starry spur, helmet on a tossing sea).
Evolving at length among the renewals
of your painted face (the goat, the ruined
columns, starlight, and turning ocean),
the constellation of most ancient light:
the dead one enormous in armor, sworn.

And after turning ocean, or starlight,
or man imperiled, you become the dead one,
standing, hefting the halberd, departing
again into the salt-stung wilderness,
where the wave goes under and you wander
armored to battle what killing thing appears:
starlight or dog or turning ocean.

THE RETURN

Was this life? Good, let it come again!
—NIETZSCHE

Did you speak those words?
But if your life were given you again . . .
—But as another turning of the maze,
or the same maze a second time;
and not the struggle you wanted,
but intricate escaping whispers
that hint (or simulate) a mystery,
and bring you (your enemy retreating,
scattered among lurkings, absences)
toward a struggle deflected
through minute, imperative clashes,
till, circling on the infinite threshold,
your weariness and your way unite;
past, future connect in a dream
there is no adversary, no ending. . . .

Yet suppose that on this
your own occluded morning
(with the wind idly revolving,
the rain oppressing the streets
with impetuous disdainful imminence),
suppose that over and over
your life returns,

mingling in a radiant moment
those turnings, those doorways and days,
your mumbled street of mazes
flashing down in the singular falls!
And you, perplexed in the roaring
of the simultaneous syllable,
go blind,
               unable to recall
the name of life
                    —as this day
(on your own cloudy morning,
the wind idling, turning,
the rain above the streets withheld)
you turn,
under the momentous, pouring body,
and search the doubtful passageways
(repeated, dividing), unaware
that from the first your cry was answered,
and your life, and lives, are here.

SCENE OF A SUMMER MORNING

Scene of a summer morning, my mother walking
to the butcher's, I led along. Mountains
of feathers. My breath storms them. Angry feathers.
Handfuls. The warm gut windings stinking.
Here, chickens! Yankel, the bloody storeman,
daringly he takes the live animals
in vain. Yankel, a life for a life! Eternal
morning too young to go to school. I get
a hollow horn to keep. Feathers, come down!
Gone. The world of one morning. But somewhere,
sparkling, it circles a sunny point.

Incredible the mazes of that morning,
where my life in all the passages at once
is flowing, coursing, as in a body
that walked away, went.
                              Who writes these lines
I no longer know, but I believe him
to be a coward, that only one who escaped.
The best and bravest are back there still,
all my Ten Tribes wandering and singing
in the luminous streets of the morning.
Unsounded the horn! And silence shudders
in the center of the sunny point,
heart-stopping at dawn.
Enormous my thieving hand in the ancient sunlight
no longer mine. Littering through my fingers,
drifting, the Ten Tribes there, lost forever.

THE PRIPET MARSHES

Often I think of my Jewish friends and seize them as they are
and transport them in my mind to the *shtetlach* and ghettos,

And set them walking the streets, visiting, praying in *shul*,
feasting and dancing. The men I set to arguing, because I
love dialectic and song—my ears tingle when I hear their
voices—and the girls and women I set to promenading or to
cooking in the kitchens, for the sake of their tiny feet and
clever hands.

And put kerchiefs and long dresses on them, and some of the
men I dress in black and reward with beards. And all of them
I set among the mists of the Pripet Marshes, which I have
never seen, among wooden buildings that loom up suddenly
one at a time, because I have only heard of them in stories,
and that long ago.

It is the moment before the Germans will arrive.

Maury is there, uncomfortable, and pigeon-toed, his voice is
    rapid and slurred, and he is brilliant;
And Frank who is good-hearted and has the hair and yellow skin
    of a Tartar and is like a flame turned low;
And blond Lottie who is coarse and miserable, her full mouth is
    turning down with a self-contempt she can never hide, while
    the steamroller of her voice flattens every delicacy;
And Marian, her long body, her face pale under her bewildered
    black hair and of the purest oval of those Greek signets she
    loves; her head tilts now like the heads of the birds she draws;
And Adele who is sullen and an orphan and so like a beaten
    creature she trusts no one, and who doesn't know what to do
    with herself, lurching with her magnificent body like a
    despoiled tigress;
And Munji, moping melancholy clown, arms too short for his
    barrel chest, his penny-whistle nose, and mocking
    nearsighted eyes that want to be straightforward and good;
And Abbie who, when I listen closely, is speaking to me,
    beautiful with her large nose and witty mouth, her coloring
    that always wants lavender, her vitality that body and mind
    can't quite master;
And my mother whose gray eyes are touched with yellow, and
    who is as merry as a young girl;
And my brown-eyed son who is glowing like a messenger
    impatient to be gone and who may stand for me.
I cannot breathe when I think of him there.
And my red-haired sisters, and all my family, our embarrassed
    love bantering our tenderness away.

Others, others, in crowds filling the town on a day I have made
    sunny for them; the streets are warm and they are at their
    ease.

How clearly I see them all now, how miraculously we are
    linked! And sometimes I make them speak Yiddish in
    timbres whose unfamiliarity thrills me.

But in a moment the Germans will come.

What, will Maury die? Will Marian die?

Not a one of them who is not transfigured then!

The brilliant in mind have bodies that glimmer with a total
dialectic;
The stupid suffer an inward illumination; their stupidity is a
subtle tenderness that glows in and around them;
The sullen are surrounded with great tortured shadows raging
with pain, against whom they struggle like titans;
In Frank's low flame I discover an enormous perspectiveless
depth;
The gray of my mother's eyes dazzles me with our love;
No one is more beautiful than my red-haired sisters.
And always I imagine the least among them last, one I did not
love, who was almost a stranger to me.
I can barely see her blond hair under the kerchief; her cheeks are
large and faintly pitted, her raucous laugh is tinged with
shame as it subsides; her bravado forces her into still another
lie;
But her vulgarity is touched with a humanity I cannot exhaust,
her wretched self-hatred is as radiant·as the faith of Abraham,
or indistinguishable from that faith.
I can never believe my eyes when this happens, and I want to
kiss her hand, to exchange a blessing

In the moment when the Germans are beginning to enter the
town.

But there isn't a second to lose, I snatch them all back,
For, when I want to, I can be a God.
No, the Germans won't have one of them!
This is my people, they are mine!

And I flee with them, crowd out with them: I hide myself in a
pillowcase stuffed with clothing, in a woman's knotted
handkerchief, in a shoebox.

And one by one I cover them in mist, I take them out.
The German motorcycles zoom through the town,
They break their fists on the hollow doors.
But I can't hold out any longer. My mind clouds over.
I sink down as though drugged or beaten.

TO THE SIX MILLION

But put forth thine hand now, and touch his bones and his flesh . . .

I

If there is a god,
he descends from the power.
But who is the god rising from death?
(So, thunder invades the room, and brings with it
a treble, chilly and intimate, of panes rattling
on a cloudy day in winter.
But when I look through the window,
a sudden blaze of sun is in the streets,
which are, however, empty and still. The thunder
repeats.) Thunder here. The emptiness resounds
here on the gods' struggle-ground
where the infinite negative retreats,
annihilating where it runs,
and the god who must possess pursues, pressing
on window panes, passing through.
Nothing's in the room but light
wavering beneath the lamp
like a frosty rose the winter bled.
No one is in the room (I possess nothing),
only power pursuing, trying
corpses where the other god went,
running quickly under the door. In
the chill, the empty room
reverberates. I look from the window.

◆

There is someone missing.
Is it I who am missing?
And many are missing.
And outside, the frozen street extends
from me like a string, divides, circles,
with an emptiness the sun
is burnishing.
                    In the street
there is nothing, for many are missing,
or there is the death of many
missing, annulled, dispossessed,
filling the street, pressing their vacancy
against the walls, the sunlight, the thunder.
Is a god
in the street? where nothing is left
to possess, nothing to kill;
and I am standing
dead at the window looking out.

                    ◆

What did you kill? Whom did you save? I ask
myself aloud, clinging to the window
of a winter day.
                    Survivor, who are you?
ask the voices that disappeared,
the faces broken and expunged.
I am the one who was not there.
Of such accidents I have made my death.

Should I have been with them
on other winter days in the snow
of the camps and ghettos?
And on the days of their death that was
the acrid Polish air?—
I who lay between the mountain of myrrh
and the hill of frankincense,
dead and surviving, and dared not breathe,
and asked, By what right am I myself?

Who I am I do not know,
but I believe myself to be one
who should have died, and the dead one
who did die.
Here on the struggle-ground, impostor
of a death, I survive reviving,
perpetuating the accident.
And who is at the window pane,
clinging, lifting himself like a child
to the scene of a snowless day?

◆

"Whatsoever is under the whole heaven
Is mine." Charred, abandoned, all this,
who will call these things his own?

Who died not
to be dying, to survive
my death dead as I am
at the window (possessing nothing),
and died not to know
agony of the absence,
revive on a day
when thunder rattles the panes,
possessed by no one;
bone and flesh of me, because
you died on other days
of actual snow and sun,
under mists and chronic rain,
my death is cut to the bone,
my survival is torn from me.
I would cover my nakedness
in dust and ashes. They burn,
they are hot to the touch. Can my
death live? The chill treble
squeaks for a bone. I was
as a point in a space,
by what right can I be myself?
At the window and in the streets,

among the roots of barbed wire,
and by springs of the sea,
to be dying my death again
and with you,
in the womb of ice, and where
the necessity of our lives is hid.
Bone and flesh of me,
I have not survived,
I would praise the skies,
leap to the treasures of snow.

II

*By night on my bed I sought him whom my soul loveth: I sought him, but I found
him not.*

*I will rise now, and go about the city in the streets, and in the broad ways I will
seek him whom my soul loveth. . . .*

What can I say?
        Dear ones, what can I say?
You died, and emptied the streets
and my breath, and went from my seeing.
And I awoke, dying at the window
of my wedding day, because
I was nowhere; the morning that revived
was pain, and my life that began again was pain,
I could not see you.
        What can I say?
My helpless love overwhelmed me,
sometimes I thought I touched your faces,
my blindness sought your brows again,
and your necks that are towers,
your temples that are as pieces
of pomegranate within your locks.
Dead and alive,
your shadows escaped me. I went
into the streets, you were not there,
for you were murdered and befouled.
And I sought you in the city,

which was empty, and I found you not,
for you were bleeding at the dayspring
and in the air. That emptiness
mingled with my heart's emptiness,
and was at home there, my heart
that wished to bear you again, and bore
the agony of its labor, the pain
of no birth. And I sought for you
about the city in the streets, armed
with the love hundreds had borne me.
And before the melancholy in the mazes,
and the emptiness in the streets,
in the instant before our deaths,
I heard the air (that was
to be ashen) and the flesh
(that was to be broken), I heard
cry out, Possess me!
And I found you whom my soul loves;
I held you, and would not let you go
until I had brought you
into my mother's house, and into the chamber
of her that conceived me.

Dear ones, what can I say?
I must possess you no matter how,
father you, befriend you,
and bring you to the lighthearted dance
beside the treasures and the springs,
and be your brother and your son.
Sweetness, my soul's bride,
come to the feast I have made,
my bone and my flesh of me,
broken and touched,
come in your widow's raiment of dust and ashes,
bereaved, newborn, gasping for
the breath that was torn from you,
that is returned to you.
There will I take your hand
and lead you under the awning,

and speak the words it behooves to speak.
My heart is full, only the speech
of the ritual can express it.
And after a little while,
I will rouse you from your dawn sleep
and accompany you in the streets.

SONG

So you are

Stone, stone or star,
Flower, seed,
Standing reed,
River going far

So you are

Shy bear or boar,
Huntsman, death,
Arising breath,
Stone, stone or star

So you are.

From MAGIC PAPERS

(1970)

MAGIC PAPERS

Before we came with our radiance
and swords, our simulacra of ourselves,
our injurious destinies
and portable exiles,
                    women were here
amid incredible light that seemed
to have no source, that seemed suspended.
And so they moved majestically,
like the months, forward without
straining, not toward their goals
yet carrying them as they went,
their round limbs seeming
to exemplify what they did,
leaning out of windows, stepping from
or through doorways, bending to uncover,
lifting on their palms, carrying and
setting down, pausing to converse,
turning to where we were not yet,
saying, Here we live the victory
of the senses over the senses.

                    ◆

Taken, hurried into exile,
excited and flushed, chosen, delighted,
the bride beckons and inclines;

Desire me! her eyes say; her hair
is combed and set in token of her reign
and servitude, her departure, her suffering.
And the day's head splits the darkness,
breaks forth, bruises her womb;
she screams; he burns and rises.
He carries a message across the sky
from darkness into darkness,
mounting furiously toward vengeance,
falling asleep so soon, and drops
the magic paper with the magic word
that falls into the chimney, into the fire
that burns the darkness, that also goes out
and no one is saved, no one the same.

◆

I remember this: the window
rinsed clear, the droplets,
rainbabies clinging there;
the day is vexed with boredom
and correction; light shining
over here cuts like a knife;
suddenly I know I will never
again be happy in my life.
They slide, they roll down in streaks of light.
Sword in hand, the crying children,
their faces bunched like fists,
storm the highest ramparts of heaven.
What else is there to do
on miserable days like this?

◆

I have lost the ability to sleep.
Conscience stabs my night through the sheet.
Murderer! He stabs again.
I feel for her, body draped in darkness,
defenseless, sobbing, trying
to sleep, trying to bring forth the day.
What is to be done?
I should have killed the bastard where he stood!

I make up a story without end.
The night is bleeding to death on me.
I have lost everything.
My open eyes keep open the night,
she clings to my lids.
Sleep would dishonor the dead;
I struggle to be born,
covered with blood my battering head,
my thought is misinterpreted.
I do not speak the language of this place.
I am innocent.
I scream.
If my voice itself could be
a stream intelligent of light!

◆

I am the father of rainbabies,
shepherd of jewels, of jews,
of boys in holiday skullcaps,
shining and white.
                    With studious rapture
I lean over their gleaming shoulders
and behold the texts of light.
What pressure holds these brilliant scholars?
The swelling unison of their breaths
expounds the lesson, Light!
They say it right!
They want to run out and play;
they shimmer, they stay,
so many! they multiply,
they dazzle, translating the glory hidden
in the chill, in the thunder of voices
from the street.
                    I tap my finger
on the pane; they slide,
they run down in streaks of light.
I rage, I cannot understand my rage.
I shake the window and splash them
into darkness.

Am I the devil?
My seed is running toward the sea.
I laugh like hell, like hell I laugh.
I am the father who cannot reach them,
I am the sons who cannot be reached
and everlasting darkness floating between.

◆

At twilight, mocking the season,
November in May is cold
and gleaming, excited, slithers,
lashing its darkness
over the glistening street;
the demon hangs in the tree,
laughing, eating the light,
then arches her body to show
her incredible extruded hole;
spewing, sucking back
her spew, pale belly up,
she lies with me like the Nile.
Conceive in me, she shrieks,
do not deny my womb!
From hole to hole, there is
no heart, harbor, nothing at all.
My word floats off, lost sail
dandled on the greasy wave.
So many scholars drowned!
Her gross tail pounds her turd
into a semblance of children.

◆

My struggle to escape the idiot,
his suckers that starve my senses,
his placental calm, his resemblance to me;
he is brainless,
he is undifferentiated,
he is always there,
he is inedible,
he is faithful to the order of things,
he has no shape,

he is obsolete,
he is slippery,
he can't even say quack.
My twin, my caul.
I refuse to be two.
Use your knife, you fool! a voice says.
The one who remains will be I,
the other is another sex.
Where I cut free, the pain in my side
surpasses understanding.
I gasp for clarification.
What is reality?
The earth leaps on me.

◆

Illness is the land for which the warriors
set out, from which return, cured, the doctors say,
of their extravagant need for reality.
The efficacy of substitutions has taught
them the existence of generalities
and boredom, that is to say, death.
They lie—the need is not extravagant,
there is no cure, I never returned.

◆

Despair is frivolous.
              Therefore
is there laughter in Sheol,
the hiccuping of drunken actors.
They vomit in their graves.

Only our shallowness saves us
from being crushed by the knowledge
of our shallowness.

What is the depth for which I thirst?

◆

I make up a story without end

of the dying child who lifts

his crippled chest, his heavy thighs;
he migrates through the earth,
hunting his lost children.
They seep, they run away.
November comes, it clogs the air,
paralytic season of rain, of chaos
and asthma. Lying on his side,
he goes white in spots like a candle;
he mourns himself everywhere
and covers the earth with his traces.
Nothing holds him; discontented,
he rolls, he plunges.

Every day in each new place, he rests
in his litter, withered and golden;
messengers flash across the heavens,
blazing with the seed they bear;
infallibly, their speed hurls them past,
but from their glowing arcs they look at him.
He sees it all: their dazzling transport,
the blue sky, their tranquil diligence,
their gaze, the seed, the sun, their breathing,
the joining of heaven and earth.
There! he thinks, there should go I.
And his sole descendants, his childish tears,
splash down and waste themselves here
on this inhospitable earth of ours.

◆

I am embarrassed. I mumble.
I blush. I am ashamed.
Before whom, stupid? Yes,
I am stupid. I look down.
I hold my hand over my mouth.
I am tongue-tied. I am too much,
I cannot.
It is comforting to be stupid,
to be confused, to look down,
to say, I do not know my name,
I am someone else's child.

I would be swept away
if I were not so burdened.
Speak to me, say
what I cannot say
that I may hear it said,
that I may say it.
I wish to unburden myself.
Kiss me. My voice
is thick, is mud,
my depth of anguish is
my depth of reservation.
I detest the wryness of my voice,
its ulteriority, its suffering
—only what is not lived
can suffer so. I wish
to give birth to the deep,
deliver myself of
this darkness, this devil.
I know the words.
I must learn to speak.

◆

After the blood,
the violence and flowing,
after conception,
the women enter the stream,
they wash and purify,
they prepare themselves;
their distended wombs, between
two waters, divide
heaven from birth.
My voice itself
a stream of light
to bathe your bodies
and behold your eyes.
Look in me! and see
what you were before
you came out of Zion
into exile
for our sakes.

THE WORD

Holding the book before his shining eyes,
he reads aloud to the prince from the sacred
texts and the profane. Clear afternoon
on an amiable terrace, beyond which: a garden
whose leisurely country gesture (its unfurling
stream, its waving boughs) companions
the ceremonious twittering of cadences

of volumes that recite, within a spreading
geography of obstacles and accidents,
the fortunes of many or two or all
parted and lost, rescued, rejoined,
of persons discovered, disguises thwarted,
random journeys toward importunate destinies,
and evil that recoils against itself
—the tales inflecting such rambling peace
as the garden discloses. All of which he reads
aloud, holding the book before his shining eyes,
while, far off, a white bird, arriving,
darts above the loftiest of the pines.

The sacred tomes, however, repeat endlessly
the one word "bread," which, with shining eyes,
he reads aloud over and over.
A bread that escapes the mouth, that dilates
in the air, transparent to the sky,
the stream, the trellised walks—so sweet,
the bread of all these, the unconsumable
one, invisible, unheard, it is
spoken bread, the uttered silence of bread
that, reverently, he reads aloud, holding
the book, as always, close before his shining eyes.

PSALM

There is no singing without God.
Words sound in air, mine
are flying, their wombs empty.
Whining for the living weight, they bear
themselves, a din of echoes,
and vanish: a subsiding
noise, a flatulence, a nothing
that stinks.
The glory of man shall fly away like a bird
—no birth, no pregnancy, no conception.

A people dies intestate, its benediction
lost. And the future succeeds, unfathered,
a mute, responding to no sign,
foraging its own fields at night,
hiding by day.
                        Withheld in the unuttered
blessing, God labors, and is not born.

But if I enter, vanished bones
of the broken temple, lost people,
and go in the sanctum of the scattered
house, saying words like these,
forgive—my profaneness is
insufferable to me—and bless, make fertile
my words, give them a radiant burden!
Do not deny your blessing, speak to us.

COLLOQUY

I have questioned myself aloud
at night in a voice I did not
recognize, hurried and
disobedient, hardly brighter.

What have I kept? Nothing.
Not bread or the bread-word.
What have I offered? Rebel
in the kingdom, my gift
has wanted a grace. I am crazy
with the brutality of it.
What have I said? I
have not spoken clearly,
not what must be said,
failed in using, in blessing.
I have wanted long to confess
but do not know to whom
I must speak, and cannot
spend a life on my knees.
Nonetheless, I have always
meant to save the world.

GIRL SINGING

The partridge, the russet bird,
lies gently on the cutting board
between the blue bowl
and the sea-green decanter.
And a young girl is singing
"A partridge in a pear tree,"
adding in a free contralto
all those increments that return
always to the partridge in
the pear tree. Perhaps she has
only now turned from the mirror
or put her diary aside,
roused unknowing by a second life
she has received from the russet bird.
It is like some genre painting
come alive with a touch of blood.
I note this without irony,

and I intend no danger.
One tress hanging down,
she bends over it as over
a baby she is going to powder.
I do not know for certain
that she is serenading the bird,
or why our spreading increments,
like a pear tree of winter,
retrace, between a bowl of one color
and a decanter of another,
the crooked steps to the russet root,
while somewhere a free contralto,
perched with two lives in an auburn tress,
clothes the tree with populous song

—as I am here in a winter scene
reasoning and yet with delight,
my voice, beyond me, conjoining
with hers in the floating air;
and it is sweet to be
the bright cold sky
in winter time and any time,
and all the snow that lies between,
and the partridge and the pear tree.

DRESSING HORNPOUT

1

The squared black massive head yanked
down draws the innards with it
and the slit skin, which droops
now, draggled, saddish coat tails.
The head has: obvious whiskers of eight
strange, curling barbels; three
nasty spines; two tiny

nearly sightless eyes. The lissome
delicious body lies exposed.
This she has done.

2

And now she ranges them side by side
on wax paper: pink little gentlemen
put to bed, with pretty tails
like raven polls fresh from the bath,
neatly combed, glistening, and stiff.
Her head tilts to one side pleasantly
for so tender and unabashed a nakedness.

3

Tidy in nothing else, a primitive
aesthetic has induced her to prod
them gently here and there toward a more
perfect symmetry. All is well!
Her smiling revery is occupied
with numbering them again and again,
for all is well.

4

Dead, still their bodies arch and flip.
Heartless, headless, in what darker,
more perilous water their wandering?
A marvelous thing!
But generally are well-behaved,
and lie still to be admired in
a wholly admirable way in their not
unattractive death. How well
they can endure being looked at!
And aptly answer her passionate gaze
by staying put.

5

Joy of the fish in his leaps,
his startled bolting, his water swilling
and low lying in the settled slime.
And other joy, of ours, in what
precipitates his narrow blood
into a less recondite, a larger
universe. Prey and morsel coincide
in death. In its relation to eating,
death is a mode of kinship, for we
are not a species that eats its food
in a tempest of wings, or wriggling,
or squealing down our throats,
yet are consanguine with all we eat.

6

Yes! the huntress returns to her lair,
dignified and wise her amble,
her mien solemn and attentive
as a courting dog's. I imagine
her quickening approach. A joyous law
hastens her stride and she is obedient.
How lovingly she carries the morsel!
It almost seems she mothers it.
The cat goes in her special trot,
a dead mouse between her jaws.
A string of tail is all that shows,
yet kitten could not be safer there.

7

And now besprinkles them liberally
—her gestures grow expansive and free—
with salt, garlic powder, and pepper,
and rolls them firmly in a coarse flour.
It is neither grueling labor nor exacting
work, and a quiet, profound pleasure.

8

A woman stands before a chopping
board, in her bloodied hands a small
cleaver. Subtly violent odor
of fish, and droplets of sweat distilled
by the heating oven, which she wipes
away with her forearm. The kitchen's
only season is summer. Somewhere
a mystery is in preparation,
but here is all the evidence.
One has done worse than fall in love
with such plainly capable hands.

FOUR PASSAGES

BRIGHTON BEACH LOCAL, 1945

Hot Saturday expands toward twilight,
Spacious and warm. Their train, at the end of the line,
Haltingly departs from Coney Island,
And settles, after an initial whine,

To a lulling commotion, with which they, too, move,
He sixteen, she almost a year older;
They have been swimming and are in love,
And sit touching and rocking together.

Exercised and sober, their bodies are
Rested, tingling, refreshed and grave, compel
The tautened skin; he is freckled,
Her complexion of the Crimea

Is healthy olive-and-rose, her frequent smiles
Transcend what is perhaps a pout or the faint
Ruminative suckling of a child;
A severe and orphan dress disdains

The completed opulence of her body. Stretching,
They vie in banter with sunburned strangers nearby,
Break off, having acquitted themselves
With honor. Pride completes their pleasure.

They are indeed proud: of being lovers,
Of their advanced and noble sympathies,
Their happiness, their languorous wit
That mocks at dignity, ripens pleasure,

And candles the failure in these faces, then
Restores their opacity with kindly justice
—Imagining their competence exceeds
Every foreseeable occasion.

These are young gods defining love, banqueting
On glances and whispered smiles and amiable
Raillery, and believe inexhaustible
Their margin for error, and summon back

The solicitous waiter, command another course
Of immortal tenderness and levity,
Drunk and dazzled with love, twining fingers
On a summer evening after the War.

Fixed in force, the train persists on the ways,
Its windows intersect the streaming darkness;
Their expanding revery engages
Almost the first apparent stars.

A cunning and subterranean will
Even now detaches them toward other destinies,
Misery, impatience, division that shall
Complete their present and mutual ignorance.

MEETING HALL OF THE *SOCIEDAD ANARQUISTA*, 1952

The rough wooden floor impedes the dancers,
Who, unable to glide, move by steps,

And, warmed by Gallo wine, gain speed, their pleasure
Neither false nor excessive, though uncertain.
Too sparse for the loft, the rest, making many,
Crowd the phonograph and wine jug on the table.

Folded chairs are ranked along a wall;
Atop the shelves, the dying pamphlets,
Absolute with ardor and fraternity,
Receive New York's gray intermittent soil,
Dust. A few Spaniards with weakened eyes
Desiccate in the fadeout of history.

Tonight, under the toneless light
Of usual selves, young friends have made
This party to welcome home a friend,
A woman fiery-looking, childless, and stubborn.
Embarrassed by gloom, she sits on the floor
And smiles her description of famine in Italy.

These two who dance have met since parting, yet,
Because she has come alone, because he, too, is,
Like one recently divorced, freshly marketable,
Novel with the glamor of commodity,
A vividness revises his elder desire,
Selects her cropped hair with loving recurrence.

Her response is rare volubility,
Her conversation challenging, obscene,
Embittered or descends to jokes or glorifies
Giving, pictures Nietzsche dying for want of love.
It is quite certain she does not like him, certain
She wishes to please. Her caricature boringly enacts

A passion genuine and chaotic. Wearing red,
At twenty-four having desired, having failed
To be reborn a Negro, Israeli, Gypsy;
Devastated by freedom, her uncompleted soul
Retains its contact with psychosis and with
The incredible softness of a woman.

Her manic vehemence drops. Dances off, gazes,
And says he looks sad, and to restore his spirits
Offers the nursery of this body she
Exhibits and dislikes; her pity and her guilt,
Like children deprivation has misled,
Hold hands tenderly, without affection.

Before night ends, forgotten at two by a mad
Mother, dragged along by her father, lodged
With orphans, she jumps, denuded, gleaming,
Nervous, from the bed, and producing
Her repertoire of wifeliness,
Asks would he like a book to read.

AT PASHA'S FIRST AVENUE CAFÉ, 1954

Three walls are tin enameled; on the fourth,
a spreading country all sienna and curves
offers in conventionally edible style,
and half-eaten already, glory that is Greece:
a bit of marzipan sitting on a hill
—it is the Parthenon; beside it, Delphi's vale
whose lovely oracle from her picnic table,
foretelling free food, expensive manners,
teaches the very gods not to grab,
while lots of girls, consuming the sun's output
of yellow, dance madly over the flowers, or caress
those half-human heads upon their human laps;
symmetrical and white, a splendid mountain
overlooks it all, though shaken, it might seem,
by inspired tremors from the artist's hand
which fluttered like a bacchant who commends
Pasha's friendly pilaf and *beautiful* wine.

Dull, but fathers, and exotic in a faintly
swarthy way, and practical about their women
who can't let anything alone with their long noses
and short fuses, and dish-busting politics,

and their big mouths and spitefulness and vanities
—vaguely indifferent, they take in the dancer's lousy
American style, from whose disorder they infer,
by casual and well-known processes, the exact degree
of her voluptuary value: how hot in bed,
and with careful Mediterranean lucidity
thank their gods she's no Greek's daughter
earning so little for showing her stuff. Roused
from their revery of sensuous shade,
they shout advice, encouragement, praise, keeping
one eye cocked at what figure they might cut
and wondering if she's maybe not there in the head.

Intolerant of the abstract ritual,
Her dancing too portentous to entertain,
Inept, overt, offensively familiar,
Breathless in the burdened unreality,

She fights toward the pure, the undemanding
Air, toward flight, aching to inspire endless
Rebirth, a plenum taut with plentitude,
Of her virgin children the virgin child; messenger

Struck dumb, nailed to the stage, staggers
Through attitudes that crazily conflate
Sexual homilies with moral coquetry;
Her gestures heave, labor to translate

The unreality: tempt, placate, challenge,
Exclude toward a universe of love and giving . . .
Unaware that her sacrifice proceeds
Beyond her power to surrender. The audience

Stirs, its attention irregular, vague,
Its judgment unfavorable, its indifference,
Like the gods', capricious but final.
The tiny uterine increments transcend

Her body: a stillness flickers, neither
Reposeful nor dancing, the emptiness

Affirms itself in repeated nothings
At one with the judgment upon her.

PARTY ON EAST TENTH STREET, 1955

    Their party has romance for its occasion,
    A courtship of roses, Saturday's roses
    Hilarious now in the violet air
    And whom the dance encounters with loves
    In a folly of poses gravely swimming, alluding to,

    Deferring always to them, though importunate
    Sometimes, begging their arms, their tresses, their kisses.
      Kisses
    Of the rose, how little they endure! consumed
    In movement, their plays revived as the air's
    Repeated caresses that pursue with music

    The weakening, dizzied roses faster, farther
    Through misleading groves of alarms and despairs.
    How cold there, frightful and lonely! till they cry aloud
    And are consoled, while the music slows, by a voice
    Lost and found in the voices of their holloing loves.

    The roses brighten and withdraw;
    look down, smooth, correct,
    amplify their persons,
    these speaking modesties
    of linen or of silk
    wherein are nursed and hidden
    the infant revelations
    whispered to their beating hearts.
    Given and giving this
    only, untouchable elsewhere
    but touched by a mothering voice,
    because of whom
    the roses love and are lovable,
    having consoled their despairs and tears,
    their fragile lament, and made coherent
    the gaze of discoursing intelligence

that dallies brightly now among the roses
and their loves, and in the party's
boisterous charade invokes
a mother invisible below
the blood that gathers at the root,
the light that wakes the flower's
flower.

What strange animals we are!
                                        Responding
to slaps and losses, teasing, kisses; eager
for contest, for smiles of shared intelligence;
witless, disheartened, drooping in solitude,
desiring sights, and the seeing of other eyes;
nourished by news and touches, crowding
the air with spirits and revenant loves;
asking of things what beings they possess;
compounding the soul of others or dividing
in a drama of voices, preferring guilt
to terror, terror to isolation.

Of hunger and thirst a king dies amid
fountains and gardens.
                              An infant, isolated
within the circling intelligence of love,
  has died.
                        What strange animals we are!
                                        Smiling
with the roses, held in their garden glances, he
receives intelligence of her, husbandless,
motherless mother. One now and now together,
they mime her gestures—goes
wandering, the infant across her arms
offered in the empty street.
Does not know how to feed it. They squeak
its little cries. Their eyes glaze. It sickens
and dies, curling like a leaf
amid their banquet of smiles.
They hide-and-seek,
cannot let her go. They clothe

themselves in her chill. Starlight
has estranged their faces.
Recurs, surviving in a stupor
beyond heartbreak, gnawing
her blue, delicate, negative
lip; she does not cry
or turn away: radiant with
no seeable light, breathless revenant
absenting in a poverty of desolation.

From such
it shall be taken to the very conclusion
of time without mercy or remission.

This one
is interesting: scrubbed pink yet oddly drab,
her articulation foreign slightly and
indistinct, direct, awkward in the dance,
stocky, broad-basined, touched with a violet glow,
and wanting, he knows, to be taken home.

Around each rose a specter glows
Bluish and biting, after the fine
Electric wit departs from it.
Odor of ozone concludes the feast
And leaves the rose its cold repose.
Spreading in darkness, the specter is the rose.

AN EPILOGUE

She has been met by others since.
They say she gardens for a living,
her manner hearty and masculine,
was married for a time, sleeps
around, though less now than before,
is given still to brooding and rages,
but faces middle age with greater
equanimity than she lived her youth,
has altered her name and has good
color, dresses better, preserves
an interest in the theater, is less
vulgar, somewhat commonplace,
and more optimistic than not.

THE FATHER

No voice declares from heaven. Must
we, too, acquiesce in the appalling
ordinariness of this man,
his heart failing and nothing to say?
Awaking, snappish, resentful, confused;
sitting with knife and fork at noon
in judgment on himself;
aching toward dinner, poor boy, newsboy,
fatherless boy, cut clean through,
dying for affection—yet proudly declining
to present his bill to his Maker
(however prudently refusing
to tear it up). One almost smiles
to read of it, although one has,
to tell the truth, sometimes
been a shit, however inexplicitly
complicit, *n'est-ce pas?*

Dying in earnest—as he was earnestly
doing—we are led to ask about
the Maker of the lion and bear,
the infinite night-shining stars,
O bright and brighter than before!
and creatures who go here and there
entangling well their various ways
on this our simple shining star.
Who is he? and by what right made us
not as we are not but as we are?
or loses us and then are neither?
And must we leave these ways, this shining,
such creatures, and the lion and bear
to his bad accounting and his inconstant care?

Humiliated, his ambitions broken,
and never, certainly, a lion at heart,
he sweetens what little he can,
tramping the low domestic earth,
hero of the hearth, the garden's guardian,

carrying the groceries in,
setting them down, brewing his own, pleased
in the pleasure of daughter and son, turning
the TV on, turning it off,
turning it back on,
punctual and solvent and undecided,
meaning none of it,
or standing dazed among the peaceful summer
greens, almost in the distance seeming
an ad's beatitude: idiot-consumer,
aging, awestruck, meek, and grateful
for the profuse and profound rightness
of all this wrongness.
                         Beyond pain,
pessimism; beyond
that, his heart cuts back
—the vise's blank ferocious fix:
fear, bewilderment, betrayal,
enmity, despotism, whatever
he swallowed or spat, all of it,
he bends and crushes together
in a powerful shrug—savagely suppressed.

I will tell you a story, it goes like this.
With waistcoat and a watch (the enormous one
that ticks so heavy, wound down
as ever and running slow), he hurries
into darkness (oh, too late! too late!)
toward a party by now long over,
the garden cleared of cakes and tables,
the little celebrants packed off to sleep
or sent out sleepily to wander
in gloomy lanes, or under hills
that slope away among stones,
led forward, poor dears! by a fictive light.
Tender and round, busy, abstracted,
everything on his mind and his mind
on nothing, quickly pleased, easily affrighted,
he hastens after, unable now
to catch that small courageous band,

hurrying badly and reeling forward,
tired, it is true, yet not disheartened
on his forsaken way where no star shines
and their laughing chatter long since faded,
faded then and reappeared, roaring in lanes
and on the hills, then reappeared, then faded.

The pain of it does not ease; this is
too much, we say, let him have known
before the end his glittering scene:
himself poised with shotgun, two yelping
beagles in a snowy field, a rabbit
never too soon forthcoming from brake
or burrow, the sky total and unexpended.

THE HEIR

He is a surgeon resectioning the heart.
Confessedly dead, yet the corpse
sits up and shouts at him, "You idiot,
do you know how to do anything right?"
And tries to grab the knife or the dream itself.
It seems to him they are struggling over
the very nature of reality.

On the bed awaking, he who was the doctor
is now the patient. So short the life, so long
the convalescence! Sad, square, and aching,
he accepts his father's dead heart, commonplace,
appalling, and the old man's misery and maiming
return in the son's chest to their brutal beating.
Devoted and good, his normality resurrects
in dull parody that bitterness and failure.

Unloaded, held to his head,
the catastrophic life clicks repeatedly
in the empty chambers.

                              Sitting in our room now
and carried away for a moment, he says, as if
repeating an important lesson, earnestly,
with yearning and with pride, "Actually,
Dad and I have the same sense of humor."

REREDOS SHOWING THE ASSUMPTION
INTO HEAVEN OF FRANK O'HARA

Farewell, sweet Pinocchio,
Human, all-too-human child,
Dead on Fire Island
Where the bad boys go
On making asses of themselves.
Death ought never have made you good
By altering your flesh to wood.

Thrust from our theater of cruelty
By a happening of fate,
The mad butch-taxi
That drove you into a state
Alien though near, too like us though far:
O supernumerary and star,
In the bright with-it summer air,
Your impromptu on surreality
Is worthy of our universal flair.
Garbed in death's sticky drag,
Out flat like a *déjeuner sur l'herbe,*
Your body's nakedness will not be late
For its brazenly touching date
With a corner of the Hamptons' turf,

While talents of the *Tout-New-York,*
Catered by a mournful museum,
Entertain eternity before
Your blue eyes' novel tedium,

And ascend from breadlines to headlines
To mumble to your catafalque
Heartfelt idiocies.
Toward cosmic in-jokes like this,
Your attitude is perfectly correct:
Flat on your back looking flat up.
You would have disapproved
Our solemn squish, but

Your spirit now, caught
In a sharp, ascending draft
And crowned with the lyric hair
Of Saint Apollinaire,
Sweeps off to Dada-glory
Amid *sons et lumières,*
Musée of Infinite Inventory
Where all pigments are a sweet
Supplice-délice,
And the lovely paintings leaning
Gaze down at our inferior world.
Lounging in open corridors,
The statues loiter to discourse
In alexandrines that beguile
The covert Muses in the peristyle.
You will write, at last, in French,
And with endless lovely women,
Fleeing their heavy husbands' exigence,
Play duets upon the piano.
Your Curatorship will be
The *Catalogue raisonné des derniers cris.*
Assemble, collate, file, remit to us,
Via pneumatiques of heaven-sent confetti,
Your final views of our sad Cosmopolis.

SEEING RED

1

Twice a week, fantastic and compelled,
Bette Davis in her latest film,
beyond the half-drawn window shade, voice
ablaze, she yanked a suitcase off the bed,
unloosed the death ray of a drop-dead stare,
the parting gusts of her furious red head.
"You'll see!" she screamed and slammed the door.
So?
    So nothing. She crept back in
and cried and fell asleep and slept.
A lion was on the landing,
a mouse was in the marrow inching.
Cornered, she poked at the burning eyes,
she spat at them, she hissed.
Fury and Misery.
The lion leaped and tore her thighs,
mice were gnawing in her feet.
A restless girl, a rotten period.

"Feh! She talks like a mocky."
                      So, my sisters
while we lie and peep across the airshaft.
Then I, like the summer dawn's ambitious sun
—eager to shine and burning to please, pink
with preference—ignite my gift for scorn
in the absence of understanding.
(Let them be praised! these red-haired sisters,
they taught my senses' prosperous bride
the famine arts of transcendence:
bitching, snobbery, condescension.
Their smell, the pale juvenile nighties,
the bloodlettings of their reddened fingernails
on passionate mornings—damp and idleness
and tempers and kicking in the tangled sheet
—brought me to a woman's country
of warmth, disorder, and cruelty,

biting envies and a smoldering shame,
so that I don't know yet if my mockery
is defending a privilege or a pain.)
My act is idiot approval that stings
her sleep. *I* am the little devil spurred
to spank those cheeks and roust her from bed,
nerves afire with sarcasm and applause.

2

One day, I think, driven as always,
she got to the door and didn't stop,
set off with her squat delirious suitcase
to wow America, or marry
—like an absentminded salesman,
his dirty wash in the sample case,
and they want it! they buy!
Who needs talent, with such despair?
What else is America for!
Bad news, bad breath, bad manners,
the grievous suitcase marches on,
prophesying from every corner.
"Betrayal!" it screams
and snaps itself shut.
What a start in life!
those scraps of rumpled underwear and clothes,
sloppy habits, bad teeth, a roaring tongue,
a crummy job and worse marriage.

3

Straddling your freckled shoulders,
riding high and sly in 'sixty-nine,
smiling (no less!) and sentimental,
each time I shift gears, underfoot
I feel your wronged hysteria
revving in the block. What
have they done to your gut?

                              Cracked
moon, homeless gingercat,

I want to take off on you,
pilgrims to nowhere,
streaking toward skid row
and failure like the vast frontier.
My young heels drum
excitedly on your tits.
At midnight you awake and cry,
My pride is injured,
my soul is empty,
my heart is broken,
my womb has died.
O my brother,
avenge me!

Rising beyond the pane,
red and pale, feverish, gaunt,
burnt crust but raw dough,
you grip your satchel
and leap through the window into
the middle of the Great Depression,
your eyes endowed with total misunderstanding.

4

Would it be too fatuous of me
and too late, too squeamish, too phony,
too perfectly American,
touching three small fingers to my brim,
to say across thirty feet of foul airshaft,
thirty years of life, "Help you with your bags, Red?"

THE WARRIORS AND THE IDIOTS

Our themes were three: defying dangers,
triumph over dangers, respite
from danger. And weapons, four: knife
and light, blood and the burning maxims:

Stain a breast before you foul your pants.
Pay twice the price, if you pay at all.
Defend father and mother, kith and kind.
These others were not warriors: ninnies
and nuts, the palsied pencil vendor,
mongolians, morons, the dwarf. Strewn about
like pumpkins, squash, or stumps grown over
with moss, they lay quietly beyond
the law, observed no imperative,
enacted no command, these children
too cruelly punished in the womb
to endure a second forfeit. Stultified
by darkness of the forty days, they had,
as if tumbled from a broken crate
or shivered constellation, rolled to a stop
in the sun, like damp oranges, like fallen moons.
Wherever we went, their grunts admonished us:
There is no victory, there is survival.
No, there is only recollection.
You think you have survived because
you can remember when you were
at once both swimming and drowning.

Even Messiah of dogs and cats
will overlook them on his final errands
through the streets, and Paradise take place
without their spoiled hosannah, they content
to remain at any angle whatever
in the sun for all eternity.

NIGHT AND THE MAIDEN

The children run away, they hide,
teasing the twilight on the leaves,
they scatter under shadows, their eyes
blink out, their voices vanish.

She follows and calls them in to sleep,
her cry impatient, but hears itself,
astonished, flirts alone, succumbs, desires
labor, desires a companion solitude,
and rises to compel the listening stars.

Toward her the stars send forth their night
—prince, husband, stranger, death—
bearer of the dark illustrious names.
He overtakes her in the wood.
She is startled by the dark pursuit,
a brilliance fallen too close.
Having come so far tonight,
leaping over all the ways,
dropping toward sleep, he draws
his darkness from the sky to light
within the empty heavens of her flesh
the lost inviolable stars.

ELEGY FOR A SUICIDE

1

Behold, these flowers of the field,
how deft they are at their windy games!
Unjustifiable, unjustified,
they are not weeping,
while you stand apart, growing thin
among the prattle of the flowers, their tidy,
childish sentences:
                    Naughty! cries the daisy.
Yes, you pumpkin! the other replies.
Will you give me one? asks the rose,
for me and Linda?
And bend together gossiping, telling
the sweet things they have eaten.

2

Feeding the children, we overcome chaos,
their eating blesses the food, blesses
the monotonous manna of our lives, feeds
our hunger for meanings. It is our commonest
form of prayer, naming the bread-word in the bread.
The blessing, too, they eat; the blessing's blessed;
eternity emerges at its growing point.

3

Tyrants, these girls convict their lives;
ruthless, humiliated beyond endurance,
will not be appeased, they want
nothing! abhor the common food,
push it away imperiously, command
a better thing, then get it themselves
from the box; their frustrated wills conjoin
with a guilt—that is a frenzy! Now
unbearable to think two thoughts at once.

4

Who is the child who will not eat?
Who knows her name? Can't she be found?
She is a secret, breakfast and dinner
preferring death; turning away,
saying nothing, unhappy child.

5

The little girls are calling the big girls
about them, for instruction, to play house
and teach them to behave—out in the backyard.
Why do you linger in a corner and won't play,
your black hair curling, eyes sullen, trembling,
thin? Ghost already? Your breath so bitter?
They want you for mother, calling in flat voices
stiff with light, Play with us! Play with *us!*

So shy of the light, you stoop to tie something
with a sudden erratic energy, hiding
your face, your fingers tighten, you drift away.
Excited, the children rush forward
shouting, Here's the baby bird again!

6

Hungry for destinies, if only
to find a crust, I follow.
Starving, if I demand of you,
will I be fed?
Past the broken ring of children
jumping in place, calling; concealed,
you lean your head on the tree,
stepmother to yourself, waif, and groom.
Gathered to bless the emptiness,
you impersonate a family,
giving, taking, in the perpetual
moment, impossible wine.
Faltering, jarred, reaching,
what do you see? Quick,
your secret, is it a destiny?
Is something fulfilled?
Louder! What are you saying?
That you're urgently, mortally *hungry?*

7

A sparrow hops to the plate.
The past is a crumb to him.
He flies away. He comes back.
He eats it, miraculous food!
Children totter at him, exploding their hands.
He flies off. A circle is completed.
They put out a second morsel.
Eternity is this crumb to him.
He possesses and divides it,
fulfilling the law.

Accursed, all parents cry
that all they have done is useless,
the unjustifiable bread unblessed!
You have cast a profaneness everywhere
but on these children, sacred for your sake.

TO WAKEN YOU WITH YOUR NAME

Almost at dawn, she babbles
the names of her childhood,
precious dolls dressed up
because they have to please:
Let go! Don't touch! Stop it!
Well, they guard her too,
though spiteful at times and nasty
and wanting always to have
their toes kissed. Tumbled hair
has touched her sleep. It is such
a little way to go . . . if the dolls
do not mislead. A breeze
feathers her hair. Hush it! Oh why
is the soul sent on errands
in the dark? with its list
of names, its fist of pennies,
its beating heart? Why, to buy
an egg, of course. See,
hen hides her egg under
the sycamore tree—smart girl!
The meadownight smiles and
rolls over in sleep. Startled,
in flight, all ears, she stares
from its edge at the old ladies
under parasols dragging
the morass of their legs.
Their smiles are tranquil and tiny,
solicit her to come

over to them. Heartbroken,
she bolts from the death-wall,
outspeeds her reckless body
that runs on its flittering shadow.
Arrow, what do you desire?
Nothing Everything Nothing
—I was born on the empty air,
cloud tops were my cradle,
and I am two, and one, and two.
To have been a child is such
responsibility—to keep
those old people from dying
you may have to stay child forever.
Who-am-I? is pretending she's
asleep, the lazy thing!
Who-was-I? makes herself
useful and carries the names
for her in a special box.
And whom will the child marry?
for marry she must. If ever
I marry, it will be
no one named in any book
ever written or read. *Who-will-*
I-be? is someone else's
doll, displeases her, she will
say a bad word to it,
and throw it down, and refuse
to look back.

To waken you, Carmen
Fidela, with your name,
I linger at your sleep's side, but
can I be gentle enough
touching you with these beams?
the day asks. And it *is*
day, called so by every chance.
Then happily the arrow climbs
to the height and sees that all
is there abiding faithfully
in the light with open eyes.

Awake, my dawn, my daughter,
sings the day, I have no
tenderness that is not you,
no distance untouched by you
idling and singing here,
for whose sake I have
abandoned the night.
I am no longer dreaming,
she says, but have I done
what I set out to do?
Both now and never,
it is you, says the day,
you and none other
entirely in this light.
Day, touch me, call me again!
she cries a second time,
for I wish to awake.

From LOST ORIGINALS

(1972)

AS FAST AS YOU CAN

Loosed from the shaping hand, who lay
at the window, face to the open sky,
the fever of birth now cooling, cooling?
I! said the gingerbread man leaping
upright laughing; the first faint dawn
of breath roared in his lungs and toes; down
he jumped running.

              Sweet was the dream
of speed that sped the ground under, sweet
the ease of this breathing, which ran
in his body as he now ran in the wind,
leaf in the world's breathing; sweeter still
the risk he was running: of boundaries first
and then the unbounded, a murderous
roadway that ended nowhere in trees,
a cat at creamspill looking up, mysterious
schoolboys grabbing.

              (Certainly they saw him,
a plump figure hurrying, garbed in three
white buttons, edible boots, his head a hat
in two dimensions.)

Powerfully then
his rhythmic running overtook the dream
of his flight: he was only his breathing.
He said, entering his body, *Like this*
I can go on forever.

Loping and leaping
the fox kept pace, hinted, feinting, over
and under wherever, licking his chops
and grinning to the hilt of his healthy gums.
Breathing to his toes the man ran faster,
free in a world that was suddenly growing
a bushy tail and a way of its own.
No less his joy for the darkening race!
Brilliant thought had dawned to his lips;
he understood it: Thrilling absolute
of original breath! and said, *The world*
desires me! Somebody wants to eat me up!
That stride transported flying him off
earth and mystic into the fox's maw
blazing. One with the world's danger
that now is nothingness and now a tooth,
he transcended the matter of bread.
His speed between the clickers was infinite.

Tell them this, that life is sweet!
eagerly he told the happy fox
whose pink tongue assenting glibly
assuaged the pure delirious crumbs.
(Others fable otherwise, of course:
having outsped our sight, he dazzles
the spinning heavens, that fox our senses'
starved pretention. How else explain
the world's ubiquitous odor
of sweetness burning and the absence of ash?)

Shimmering and redolent, his spirit
tempts our subtlest appetite—there he runs!
freely on the wind. We sniff a sharp

intelligence, lunge and snap our teeth
at the breathable body of air
and murmur while it is flying by,
Life is unhappy, life is sweet!

THE *TITANIC*

Secret in a woman's coat, her hat,
his face hidden by a veil, crazy
with fear and shame there among women
and children shivering in the boat,
he escaped huddled over an oar
on the cold and coldly misted sea.
His last sight was the deck awash and screaming.
Sick to the depths of his stomach,
he retched on the gray Newfoundland shore
and drowned in the bitter syncope.
Under a hovel roof, he woke
naked in a woman's arms and could
remember nothing, having become
what henceforth he would call *himself.*

One hundred fathoms down, withdrawn
from every future and larger than life,
with nothing left to lose or wish, the Titans
sit in their eternal afterglow
and with glorious instruments—
curving, belled, and fluted, the fruits
of a golden age—blow upward,
in vast unison and bubbling serenity,
toward the solemn void, the dizzying precipice,
Nearer My God to Thee!

MY OLSON ELEGY

I set out now
in a box upon the sea.
—MAXIMUS VI

Three weeks, and now I hear!
What a headstart for the other elegists!
I say, No matter! by any route and manner
we shall arrive beside you together.
Envy, Triumph, Pride, Derision:
such passionate oarsmen drive my harpooneer,
he hurls himself through your side.
You lie and wait to be overtaken.
You absent yourself at every touch.

It was an adolescent, a poetboy,
who told me—one of that species, spoiled,
self-showing, noisy, conceited, *épatants,*—
voice breaking from the ego-distance like
a telephone's, not a voice indeed
but one in facsimile, recon-
stituted static, a locust voice,
exhumed, resurrected, chirring
in its seventeenth year, contentedly
saying, "And I've just completed
section fifteen of my Olson elegy."

Landscape on legs, old Niagara!—all
the unique force, the common vacancy,
the silence and seaward tumultuous gorge
slowly clogging with your own *disjecta,*
tourists, trivia, history,
disciples, picnickers in hell;
oh great Derivative in quest
of your own unknown author, the source,
a flying bit of the beginning blast,
sky-shard where early thunder slumbers:
the first syllabic grunt, a danger,
a nameless name, heaven's tap on the head;
you, Olson!, whale, thrasher, bard of bigthink,

your cargo of ambergris and pain,
your steamy stupendous sputtering
—all apocalypse and no end:
precocious larvae have begun to try
the collected works beneath your battered sides.

See them now! dazzling elegists
sitting on their silvery kites on air
like symbols in flight, swooping daredevils
jockey for position, mount a hasty breeze
and come careering at your vastness
to read among the gulls and plover
—but the natural cries of birds do not
console us for our gift of speech.
Embarrassed before the sea and silence,
we do not rise or sing
—wherefore this choir of eternal boys
strut and sigh and puff their chests and stare
outward from the foundering beach.

King of the flowering deathboat, falls,
island, leviathan, starship night,
you plunge to the primitive deep
where satire's puny dreadful monsters,
its Follies and its Vices, cannot reach,
and swim among their lost originals
—free, forgotten, powerful, moving
wholly in a universe of rhythm—
and re-enter your own first Fool,
inventing happiness out of nothing.
You are the legend death and the sea have seized
in order to become explicable.

—Smell of salt is everywhere,
speed and space burn monstrousness
away, exaltation blooms in the clear:
fair weather, great *bonanza,* the high!
—swelling treasure, blue catch of heaven.
The swimmer like the sea reaches every shore.

Superlative song levitates from lips
of the glowing memorialists,
their selves flash upward in the sun.

Now you are heavier than earth, everything
has become lighter than the air.

HUMP

Arriving at last, he threw down the burden from
his back, his hump, the mailpouch his father.
Well, he thought, straightening, *these* letters
will never be delivered, unless themselves they go.
As if in answer, glittering and quick,
as white as milk, the ancient promises dove
into the pores of the ground.
                              Hump stayed put,
fuddle-fardel changed and changing.
It made him laugh and weep to see
his heap: marvelous callosity
of passed possibles and plenty's
opalescent horn, the little fluxflocks,
oh made him weep and cheer to hear
love's lithe youngtongue's shaping song

mouthoozemuse
titwitwoostalk
stablebabelburble
mamadrama
murmur-butt
plum plump lump bump
mud-udder
underhump of moo-maid
clod of milkmud, of claycud
tongue of muddlemodeler spoon and spade

babyshape
so tender to touch: smother sup
sleeperslupper
bloomballoomboom
sayseedsomescatterthing
thunder lung
a ling a ling am
goat goad 'em scrotum
god prod in pod
rosey ring
hole hilly high light
skyskullscald
and down fall all!
humpty-thump in sulph-muddlepuddle
           in self-meddlepedal
           in silt-middlepiddle
dauphin-coffin
tumblestone and rubblebone
apocalumps
all out! all off!
and all groan up!
           Last leaped forth
leathery, wizened-wise, he, Humpback self,
and stood curved, panting before him as if
from long labor, then stoopingly strutted,
confronted, while himself tender touching
and frotting a bald spot frayed on his back.
He saw the Hunch was tiny as a child,
aged as a sire, cackling as a goose, crackling
as fire, tricky as trouble is was he,
manjock grizzled, fizzled, fiercer-farcer,
stick stuck in earth, bent body C,
and held a bag of pennies, held a key.

So that is what you look like, he addressed
the humped one. Who are you? My father are you?

You who are, impostor?
What have done with son,
child of dreams, child I would have been?

Father, he I am, that very child!

Then I'll eat you up, you worstwurst, you father
-fodder, huffed the gnome, puffing and swelling
and showing the sharkshead that grew from his back.
For I am thy father-farter, thy thunder-thudder!

Eh? Say again! I dare.

                    I am die fudder
-flooder, die dunder-dudder, die blooder!

And my sputter spitter! How could runt you
eat me giant? he asked his father.

If no respect, no, oh pity then me
who need a thousand years to straighten back,
so long have bent at dismal diking,
abandoned, alone, and none relieves,
bitter nights bright days, wanting wee,
waters within, without, withholding.

Not shamed you seen such bad posture?

Now tears he could not withhold.
Many they were, obedient to gravity.
O better I had never been born!
bitter I niver bin bone, 'lone and muvverless on erf!
His numbed lips could scarcely make the sounds.

If father curses life, what shall son say?
Nothing. So said he never and never.
But hunchback held not his peace:
Pursuing future, dreaming self,
half of you has been desire,
other half, conceit,
but desire does not savor always,
sweet conceit sours in its season.
Bitter bastard, do not deny me, do not

refuse my legacy! I am your father
and your father's fathers. I am your key,
crouch on my here heap, this hump
of refuse, wreckage, scurf. Pisgah my.
Sinai. Moriah my. My Ararat.
Foresee I promised earth, son and city. Way
is narrow, is hard, passage difficult,
wince will you going through. Go, too, I
may not, help shall, save you maybe,
am key.

He touched the hunchback's back and found it ridged
like the frozen sea. Indeed, he was the key.
Quickly he turned him in the lock then.
Key melted, and hump broke
and stone broke, the river ran by.
Briefly he saw blue eyes bubbled, floating
on the water, their gaze of pain, puzzlement,
eternal shyness too too much to say goodbye.
And wild water's mouth sucking itself down, drowning,
shouted, Save yourself, you sonofabitch,
but save me too, save our family, our history!

Stooping he drank the knowledge that flowed
at his feet like a mountain stream, so cold,
so strong, so pure it humbled and broke his mouth,
stung his ears and stopped his heart
like sentence of death: the taste
beyond spitting out, extenuation,
of his unmitigable mediocrity.

He knew then he was not free,
but of what he was not knew not,
nor to what end or why.

THE JUMPING CHILDREN

The field is lively with children. Although it is night and sleep is commanded, they are awake, linked perhaps in secret to the antipodes, the day. Dressed in the styles of forty years ago, like discontinued angels, they do not move forward or back, they are jumping, crying as they rise, I want to be, I bet myself! singing as they sink, I am my point of repose, no other.

These, who have just begun to master the simultaneous leaping and wing-beating, repeat their abrupt impromptu floppings like dancers warming up who take off without apparent cues, collapse before completing the arc; while others, as if testing the ground underfoot, hop a bare bit, never exceed the measure, come down with patient zeal.

Some jump higher and higher, bounding up in great leaps, their little throats swell like gulls', they soar and sing. The joy in descent is no less than the leaping, their concentration is absolute, their fall is flying. Afoot, they lift their knees like runners after a race, half-bend from the waist, and windily shake their dusty cloth wings on the clattering wire frames.

The cripples with withered legs, with powerful crutch-wielding shoulders, who—if they were actual children—would have scuttled after the crowd of racers, one side dragging, the other leaping forward, jump now in eager hobbled verticals, balancing on useless legs until their arms take hold and lift them from deformity.

The children with the largest pinions leap lowest, endure longest, appear in their endless hovering hardly to move at all, comets whose flight so far exceeds a lifetime they seem never to absent the sky, as though they attended an unending revelation.

These others flex knees and drone until their heads reverberate with the sound of motor flight, suddenly their chests' marvelous din lifts them before their legs can spring.

Unaware of the power of fragility, little hunchbacks, with their mysterious conformity to invisible circumstances, crouch and hop on one leg only.

Jumping is a pleasure, a mystery. And it is exciting to be among so many. Breathing the space, they refine themselves, each becomes his single substance. Straining, he leaps, his leap overtakes him, jumping lightly on to his shoulders.

Now they are bounding in the beautiful dark interim, eager to jump from the embrace of your fantasy, to be actual children who press bright bobbing faces against the high windows and peer into the darkened room, where you lie in bed imagining their ebullient society. Even now, they crowd the street at your door, call you out with irresistible greetings.

THE DAY

If Eden ever was, it cannot now
be seen, obscured by what is certain:
the treasure of our wakefulness,
its aura we have called the day,
these vivid shards that are our daggers,
these gleams we strike against the dark,
a vastness of slivers outshining
the plainness, the clarity,
the pleasure of Eden.

Gazing deeply at, but never into,
the bright impenetrable bits, too densely
bright, we cannot enter, cannot break
them smaller—our gaze is halted by
their perfect whiteness of frozen fire—
we sense the pain of their cramming in,
immurement, of, then, their exudation,
as it seems, of light, how powerfully
they wish for wholeness now if only
in commingled radiance!—we sense
the pain of this desire, of all desire,
we feel their kinship to us, we say,
The day was made for us, we are the day.

No farther on we see, no farther back,
our blindness, the visible world concur:
nullity of everything less brilliant than
these shatterings of our lost terror
—the flaming swords of those gods those heroes
who, desiring us and our desire, came
and burned Paradise to the ground.

MORTON'S DREAM

Dying, Morton saw a child who was
the child he'd been, who would become
the man he is, now almost no longer
is—already the boy's shoulder had
huddled subtly forward as if it cradled
a heart attack, some incurable effort
at perhaps an impossible freedom;
he seemed, bright against the subtracted
dark, to have banished every background.
Then Morton understood the missing world,
the hidden heart attack were one.

Could he have stopped him, crying out,
"You, go back! for out of every
possibility, you alone will die"?
His throat was glued shut. The child
no less pursued him, loomed forward, soon
would be as large as he, soon be him.
Or would have waved him off . . . but the boy,
helpless or too resolved, made no sign,
did not stop. Then Morton touched crushed hand
to broken mouth and sucked the pain it held,
and huddled in mourning for the child—
father, son, himself, his heart, which?

—missing forever from Paradise.
Culpable, the bitterness of his shame
united with the mystery of death
in something he could only call hell.

Behind a high overshadowing wall, dark,
barred, forbidding—surely that is
Eden, he thought—he heard the creatures
he had refused to be, harelip, crocochild,
calf's head, lung, shy imperfect beasts,
carouse, thump, groan, mutter coarse
unwordable noises, strangled gutturals
that shuddered in him as if, deep within,
a giant hand were slamming doors.
He thought, If I could see them once again
I might not die. So great his yearning,
one door stayed open a crack, a slit . . .
quickly all of him slipped through.

THE MARVEL WAS DISASTER

1

Aboard the wreck, passengers crowded
the windows, peered out. And saw
a band of children struggling in the surge
of a purely green and sunlit field.
How amazing the field's swift flow
forward, and that children had appeared
plunging toward them at its farthest border!
And they, happy to forget their obvious
wounds, were thinking, So, we are wrecked
relative only to all the rest, with which
we no longer keep pace, no longer desire!
Forgive their error, they desired so much

—how else could they be dying?—and yes,
they heard far off the children courageously
singing Courage! to their reviving hearts.
See there! see there! they shouted inwardly,
each gesturing in his throat to a child
overwhelmed and farther off than ever
but pressing toward them with all its might.
Nonetheless, in thought at least and blindly,
they were leaping forward for the rope
the distant hands held out . . . leaping
for a point a world at last
without direction.

2

The children who came across the field
to gawk at the fabulous disaster
found it toppled in a dry ravine,
its forwardness collapsed, its body
smashed open, rusted out, gutted;
inside it nothing, stale emptiness,
the smell of old air in a tire—unless
the little babble they thought they heard
was cries of children crying out, or beating
of something, a heart, hidden, marvelous.
Swiftly the marvel was disaster.
Within the wreck, a whirlwind
blew up their lungs,
and looking out they saw the pasture:
a garden of cut gestures, blown away,
crushed in the sudden distance
—little bridge, bright morning, themselves
standing there, dwindling
in the infinitesimal splendor,
a pinhole blazing lost light.
No star can bring it back!
At this speed, in this darkness, they know
they won't get out again, ever.

X

am I speaking to you
    yes

are you listening to me
    yes

what time is it
    it is too early to say

how early is that
    before the bird,
    before dawn

is it dark
    yes

what is that
    your breathing

and that silence
    that is silence

where was I
    with darkness, death
    far away

and how did I come here
    breathing,
    asking questions

is it still too early
    yes,
    I cannot say yet

why can't you say
    I must listen

ought I to be frightened
    no,
    you must not be frightened

shall I go on asking questions
    I cling to your voice

will that be very long
    yes,
    not longer than you can endure

and then what will happen
    I shall say you are my child,
    the dead will arise

at dawn
    at dawn

and will I have my things back
    I don't know

will I want them still
    I don't know

what were they
    your toys,
    your tribe

why did you give them away
    you were dying,
    I thought so

was that right of you
    wrong,
    bitterly wrong

did I cry
    I don't know

why do you say I don't know
    I don't know

are you being honest
    I don't know,
    no

what time is it now
    dark

and will I have children of my own
    they will be numberless,
    they will name you in their prayers

will I hear their prayers
    you will hear them
    listening for you

is that what you are doing now
    yes,
    I am praying

will you be my child
    yes,
    if I can

what is my name
    you will know it

will I remember that I was dead
    as in a dream
    only

where am I now
    near me,
    near my ear

am I as close as that
    yes,
    closer

but why am I dead
    I cannot say that

won't you tell
    I am afraid

did you kill me
    yes

were you alone
    yes,
    there were others

why don't you speak louder
    I am afraid

who were they
    very many

and am I alone
    no,
    you are many

who
    father
    fathers
    son
    sons
    brother
    brothers

why should I be born again
    I cannot live without you

are you also dead
    yes,
    I am dead

will you be born again
    I think so

are you me
    yes,
    also

will I have to stay a child
        I don't know,
        I don't think so

will I have a body then
        yes

where is my body now
        lying
        in a field
        on a hill
        near a tree

will I forgive you
        yes,
        I am unforgivable

why
        you will hear my prayer

and then I will assent
        I don't know
        I think so

why will I assent
        I don't know

and am I messiah
        yes

and messiah is a dead child
        yes,
        from the dead kingdom,
        hunting his children

and will I find them
        I don't know

and will I come to you at dawn
        promptly

and you will be here
    yes

and you will assent to my return
    I will try

and will you succeed
    if I hear the words

what are they
    I don't know,
    my words

what is assent
    my heart overflows

will my heart overflow
    with light,
    yes

may I sleep now until it is time
    I cannot endure
    not to hear you

will you continue to listen
    yes,
    that is my prayer

and you will hear
    breathing,
    you,
    I think

can you say more clearly
    no

will you wake me in time

BIRTHDAY

And arrives where all are strangers, all
are kind. He thinks, We are familiar, surely,
since they are kind, and yet seem strangers
—or I am someone other than I think,
myself the only stranger.
                          They come close
now with smiles and offerings, with large
sounds, with faces luminous and vague,
with gestures inviting one to sit down,
to dine, to take one's ease, to stay
among them or, if one chooses, to leave
in peace, but later, later on. He thinks it
endlessly, teasingly perplexing; he asks,
Whom do they find so lovable? Someone
they are awaiting? Am I that person?
And believes himself an impostor
imposing, a grabber of gifts intended
for others, but senses afterward
how impersonal their kindness, how
profound their courtesy, that they should
have greeted him as brightly had he been
any other.
            This is reposeful, a final
kindness, a tact, not to require response
and answers. If there was another life,
he hardly remembers it now, or if
he came this way on a particular
errand, and cannot declare for certain
this is the place he started for.
His gestures mean to say *No matter,
I will not oppose your kindness or stay
estranged or go away from you ever.*

RUE GÎT-LE-COEUR

Come look at the girls, said Edward
from the window, *rue Gît-le-Coeur*.
We ran to look.
Storeys down, some black queens
stood shrieking in the street. Then
the burble of Paul's tolerant chuckle
accompanied their disfigured joy; then
two Arab boys drifting through the flat
as through remembered desert, it was
as dry almost, as dusty as that.
At noon another—ex-student of
the medical fac—could be seen
waking in a farther room: some
swarthy figurine washed up among
the dingy rivulets of a sheet,
rubbing sleep-sand from his eyes
with fragile dirty fists.
Half old pasha, half mamma,
Edward pottered in a tattery robe,
emptied ashtrays, vaguely dishragged
a table, childlike handed 'round
bits of Dada curios in polyglot,
clippings, photos, collages of
outmoded monsters, broken, twisted limbs.
Someone said it made him think
of shreds of Greeks hanging, heaped
in the cyclops' cloaca-eye-and-maw,
the roaring cave's dark doorway. Speaking
of Greeks, Paul, tamping his pipe
with a scorched thumb and puffing, explained
about the war between the gods of earth,
the gods of air, the former smouldering,
blasphemous, full of spite, the latter
quick, arrogant, deceitful, thundering.
Was this place a pinnacle or hell?
Babel, perhaps. Hell on high.
Now we could smell the darkness in our light.
At two, the psychoanalyst from Lódź

came in, years and years out of Auschwitz,
a neo-nihilist loaded with matches
from the holocaust. Little flames
leaped from his coat, from everywhere
about him, his eyes gleamed, his forest hands
rubbed cracklingly together and he laughed,
certain that nothingness would be
preceded by fire, and every brilliant
horror have its utterly dark sabbath.
In that faith, he glanced around the room
and rested.

THE TENOR

The tones are pure,
                    but in his mouth, too much
too long in use, you hear the surging gangs
of children at their grimy murderous game.
They kick up dirt with their heels; they shout, defy,
accuse, drop to a knee and take deadly aim
while their stuttering throats slam bullets out;
when they win, joy careens and smashes through them
like a speeding car out of control; defeated,
they bluster and brood, deflate, droop; they cheat
too often; caught, they jut their jaws, grab for more;
they moralize, they give the raspberry, the finger,
they whisper, mutter, backbite, consume, secrete,
they swear and forswear and bear false witness;
their bickering and deliberate quarrels
wreck the game; furiously, they begin over,
hurl themselves into play with the abandon
of bursting pods; they scatter; they change sides
with swift and passionate righteousness.

Meanwhile, he is singing away
as if there's no such thing as history.

His eyes roll up for the high notes in little
mimicries, he stands on his toes.
The butterfly blue heavens escape
the mile-high nets, something
flickers on the heights, something
not itself not anything else
disappears.
                    Down
in the mouth, wanting
to shove the kids aside,
his tongue flops fuzzily,
caterpillar from the green leaf blown.
It's all *bel canto* and mucky shoes.
You can taste every lozenge he ever sucked.
Gallons in the salons.
Mouthwash carbona cologne beer steam starch.
The fraying vocal apparatus in the closet
is an old waiter's black suit:
stiff with habit, stands at attention, knees
bent, hand held out, pockets distended;
one cuff in the soup, one foot in the gravy;
worm wants it; dog
daunts it; cat kittens on it.
Song?
He mourns mewfully.

If only the world had one unadvertised pleasure!
—and one unmentionable terror!
and one note free of every melody!
he could spit those children out and shut the shop
and live happily humming till millennium comes,
should anything be worth the saving.

OUR LEADERS

No longer troubling to charm, curt,
without cadence, they bark their lies,
impatient of our credulity,
like teachers who repeat the lesson
for idiots stuck on the first page.
They pity themselves, complain
our stupidity forces them to lie,
and say *Why can't we do as we please?*

Their guile, complaints, their greediness.
Capable of nurture only, we
are like mothers, we nourish them,
believe what they say and repeat it
for one another, knowing the while
credulity isn't enough
and something not easy is required,
a pretense of intelligence,
a sacrifice, a faith they could believe
worthy of their treachery, worth
betraying. It is adversaries they crave,
and what lies we think we hear are
higher truths we have overheard.
                                But nights,
the children sitting in a ring, we take up
the papers, speak aloud the pathos
and mystery of our leaders' lives.
Alone, in dark chambers, in ordinary-
seeming chairs, at the innermost recession
of a thousand thoughts, they reach decisions,
while wives bring warmth and grace and wit
(we venerate their warmth and grace and wit)
when they are tired or under the weather,
servants trot softly in the hallways
with urgent whispers, vehement faces,
and only with the utmost diffidence
their dogs roll over—lips in rictus,
eyes alert, little paws held up like sticks
—begging to have their bellies scratched.

To know this is a constant pleasure!
Then, to move our coarse fingers along the lines,
over the inscrutable words, to murmur their names,
to feel ourselves becoming more human,
to draw close about the fire!
                    At such moments,
overcome by shame for our clamorous natures,
we look down, our eyes seek out the children,
we see their small heads, unimaginably
like ours, bent above the pages, the furious
concentration that grips their innocent
unblemished faces, their minds that leap ahead
to seize the ending before the tale is done.
This generation, we say to ourselves,
they will be different, *they* will be better!
Powerfully, they bend our eyebeams to themselves
—we see, we *feel* them bending within
our unbreakable domestic circle.
This is awesome, this is more than sweet.
And what would life be without affection!
—it is our solace, our achievement,
it is the language we speak.
It says that everything is true.
And truly, as we disbelieve less, the world
becomes miraculous beyond believing,
though less a place requiring us, less, at last,
our own.
                    The thought of our nonentity,
the world without us, this large bare ball
flying empty into the empty day,
is stunning, takes our breath, like something
intimate and alien, like a knife
in the lungs.
                    Our leaders chide us,
for sentimental, for living in others,
but can they guess our helplessness?
We break another stick from the ramparts
and thrust it on the fire set blazing
by all the power of our affection
—and another necessary lie comes

quiet from the matterless night, settles
panting beside us, warms a bloody muzzle
between paws, snuggles down toward sleep.
So everything ends, like this, near a fire
in silence and wonder, our fingers idly
soothing a murderer's nape, and somewhere
out there, a last bitter scream doesn't stop.
They don't bother stifling it,
even with a lie.

MEETING IN LYON

The winter night gives birth before me, it is you
hurrying from the mists of Lyon
between the New Hotel and Place Carnot:
shock of dullish hair, widow's peak,
dead uncle's baggy suit, dead nephew's
bursting coat, dirty collar, varicose tie,
suitcase so torn you've webbed it with cord.
In broken French you ask for the bus to Bordeaux.
In broken French I answer, crying out
That way, sir! with confident misdirection,
never dreaming you'll go, yet off you rush,
limping grandly, swinging your free elbow.
What business could *you* ever have in Bordeaux?
Might as well ask for the bus to Budapest,
the bus to Chicago! Oslo! Maracaibo!
Why kid me, a stranger in the street, asking
for outlandish places, pretending
a life to live and all that says,
history, property, people, god,
that whole landscape of the arbitrary
to give you breath, to call you darling!

And so you go,
country on your back, selves in a satchel,

a cipher becoming the century.
Powerless, you do nothing, recur,
like a myth, echoing around the corner,
stepping off boldly on the wrong foot
toward the empty provinces of rain.

A BALCONY IN BARCELONA

For Madeleine Morati-Schmitt

1

Space abstracts the body, and the eye,
more avid, reaches toward some clinging point
way way off. But it is the twilight,
gentle and victorious as an undertaker . . .
O there are weeping mysteries here, something
I knew that I've forgot, some creature-thought
yawning its drowsy dim way to the lap
of a little cave. At times like these one feels
suddenly one has misplaced the whole sky.
Now hill and sea are asleep in caves,
and far away the ancient port lights up
and little roads on the slope are lit and go
floating off in the dark immensity.
More, more lights! cries the eye demanding only
the impossible. Grand burial in the air,
the stars in procession—is it my body there,
my eye following it aloft over the city
and over all and on and out of the world?

2

With so much sky there's so much weather. It's
like being at sea, where the day's wind or sun

are a destiny filling all the time till sleep.
"Looks like rain today," which won't be the same
as yesterday's. Today's weather is today's.
There is no other news on the balcony
but what comes drifting down from above, rain
today, tomorrow sun. We're that close to the gods,
who speak in elements and have no other
business but leisurely conversing, charming
the sky with bolts, with clouds, with subtle
pituitary whispers and large vascular
digressions. Our bodies listen, brought always
to the same postures at the railing to gaze
with the same powerful vague intent. Rain
it is today! A rainy day in Barcelona
is all the rainy days the world will ever need.

SIX SAILORS

To Pete Foss,
God give him good berth!

Shipped deckhand June of 'fifty-one
aboard the *Willis Van Devanter,*
chartered to Union Sulphur and Oil
(stack colors dull ochre, black)
and carrying coal from Norfolk out
to Dunkerque, France, on the Marshall Plan
—old Liberty de-mothballed in Baltimore,
shaken down, painted over, and papered
with a pickup crew, scourings of the seven
saloons of Hoboken, Mobile, Camden, Pedro.

Here we are, bosun, carpenter, watches. Jake,
Cox, Wally, Slim, Chips, the Finn, myself,
Ole, Moe, Chris the Dane, Pete Foss, bosun,
average sorts of monster, more or less:

brawler or bragger, wino, nut, nag,
bully, slob, simpleton, thief,
this carp of leaden contempt,
this john aspiring to mackerel,
these sponge, crab, clam,
bottom-feeders almost to a man,
lungless on land, finless afloat,
sifting the margin of muck
with sodden sense and cramping gut.
Adrift in wide iron belly
amid tall waves always at world edge,
sailors are liable to misadventure
into monstrosity, forgotten
elsewhere, lost to themselves.
                                        Near
mutiny, storms at sea, quarreling
drunks, fistfights, a broken screw, two
stowaways, a crewman's fiddle stolen, heaved
overboard or hocked, kangaroo court and Moe
condemned to dine alone for dirtiness,
Wally of the middle watch busting open
lockers, out three days slugging hair tonic,
shaving lotion, as if the stuff were scotch,
Lulu and a second whore clambering
over the barges and hustled below
before the ship had ever touched a dock.
These the adventures, nothing legendary,
just "adventures," nothing more, anecdotes
from someone else's less-than-war.
                                        Otherwise,
our common peaceable humanity's
old routine: chipping gunwale rust,
soogeeing the wheelhouse down, bow watch
under the stars, the coffee pot perking
day and night, the binnacle's hypnotic
click-click-click, meals and meals, cards
in the mess, Pete Foss's lined face pokered
around his pipe, sunning out on the hatches,
winch work, fire drill, boat drill,
endless talk of sex, endless trivial

housekeeping chores of homeless householders
wandering on the wide wide sea, sleep
in the throbbing, rolling, roaring, yawing, shivering tub.

Each from his isolation, each
from transmogrification,
his little pleasure
or lengthy sleep,
a sudden gracing woke;
the mast, our common labor,
a confluence of task and wave,
of waves blown into wind,
the one, the pure transparent day
brought us there together.
At the infinitesimal intersection of these historic enterprises,
commercial, national, imperial,
within an indefinable cosmic
context, six of us climbed the mainmast
with beaknosed hammers, buckets of paint
to scrape it clean, to make it new.
Gulls dove, dolphins rolled,
sun swam ahead on the sea,
and we wind-jockeys on bosun chairs
in our thrilled community
let lines go and flew, out around
the dancing lodgepole of the turning sky
that first and dazzling morning of the world.

BEMBÚ A SU AMADA

A María Luisa Pedrosa de Alexandrino y Zaira Elisa Del Olmo

She says, "Bembú"* (my cognomen, surname,
Panache, alas!), "poet named too well for lies,
Get out! I will not look at you again!"

*Big lips.

She climbs the haughty tower of her wrath
And with a final imprecation casts

Herself naked on the roaring wind.
Dido reigning amid the raging populace
Of her pyre was not half so glorious
As you are stamping your foot on the floor.
My anger fizzles, admiration flares.

By the sainted mother who bore you,
Your worthy uncles and lamented father,
Solid men of esteemed position,
Merchants all of Iberian delicacies
And local products of the highest caliber

Sold in two suburban branches
And in the main store off the Plaza,
O redolent heiress of Park Provisions,
Pensive or busy at the counter
In the cool green depths among the jars

Of saffron, cinnamon, and chili peppers,
The monster cheeses, the Asturian *cidra,*
The pickled parts of *toros de lidia,*
And tins with scrollworked, gilded labels,
Fine testimonia of kings (kings in exile

Or dead long since from natural causes,
Whose fluttering spirits haunt, blue ribbon
In a bluer hand, the fairs of a fairer day)
—Reflect on those dusty lightless monarchs,
Their proper queens alongside thinking hard

Of dignity and their estates, with skirts
Of stone on stony knees, their consorts,
Loyal in death, loveless and unappealing!
And do not suffer your lovely ear's abuse
By what those whisperers impute to me!

As I respect your blessed mother,
Your uncles and the family business,
The lace that hems your bourgeois slip,
The droplets gleaming on your tender lids
While you complete the inventory

Or verify a bill of lading, know,
If I could tell you in my voice itself
And not in this impersonation,
I would say I love you all
Beyond approach or approximation.

That I am Bembú, bohemian, poet,
Posturing vainly in the public face,
Have given all my sighs for publication
And your heavenly tears to the dreadful cheeks
Of poetry readers—forgive me, *nena!*,

For I cannot, yet cannot change my purposes.
And what is any other but a pale
And seeable moon burning with the beauty
Of your almond eyes so fierce and sweet
I am blinded if I look one minute!

Too timid to be Homer, for all my mad
Ambition, brightening his night with song
Singing *that* denied his eyes' possession,
I glance aside. The meager sights
Starve my eyes' continual craving.

That flaming day they took you from me
In their shiny flatulent car, the gloomy
Folk of your family crammed among,
You continued smiling with exceeding
Joy, my heart has not altered to this day.

Wait for me at noon before the store
And I shall escort you in the streets
Of gossips who joylessly contest with tongues,

Those files of envy scraping harmlessly
As cricket legs on the gates of heaven.

We will go the long way 'round, and by
The roundest way return. You shall be seen
To take my arm, I to incline my head.
By these signs we shall be known
Those unknowable noons when the star

Is burning and stillness both
And both in our sufficing shade.

Translated from the Spanish of Juan Díaz Bembú,
born in Corozal, Puerto Rico, in 1933

THE TWO

Hidden everywhere,
they are two, are
twins, are husband wife,
scrolls turning to offer,
turning to take, and lie
in gradual quiet speaking,
asleep and waking together,
waking to one another
at night, both one and
divided, sky and earth,
beginning end. How
strange! How near! they say,
the one and the other,
Be my light, be
my darkness, my sleep,
my waking!
I will!
I am!

TO S., UNDERGROUND

Conceit is not news,
vanity not news,
nor the jaunty cripples of a season,
impresarios to their famous
lyrical humps.
                    And yet
these thoughts keep me awake, or I
awake to keep such thoughts,
insomnia striving
between shame and envy, saved
by neither from neither, between
nihilism and indignation,
beleaguered by both.

But there you are
with a mailing list and three forgotten volumes,
your toe in the door of forty,
faithful to failure—childhood's eternal
province—hard times' new hero
in a last corner of the old place,
sniffing the ancient culture of spilt milk,
living lean in a fat time,

my friend,
of indefinite gestures
that wave the light away,
of smiles of stymied gentleness,
of patient carbons,
your black virgins going gray
but keeping in touch,
and puns that go nowhere punctually,
obsolete timetables
of your misery,
your autumn anthologies
shuffling the loose leaves,
your little flame,
your sadness,

your embarrassed tongue,
old porter fumbling bags,
all unspeakably too much to bear.
You gaze out, and nothing there
dissuades you from your privacy.

S.,
it tempers my mind to think of you,
your tiny vortex, its peaceful dwelling
like water on a drain, dauntless
and quiet, spinning, creative, stooping
to scan the humblest darkness
with diffident clarity;
you are gentle and do not weary
and persist for failure, carrying
your small debris around
and around—the lightest things
the deluge left—and you drop
toward its deeper issue, imagining
the earth's unenunciated
still there where your paradise drowned,
the tribe of lost aboriginals,
thick, buried deep, dumb roots
in a place of restoration.

And so you put children together,
wittily, out of whatever: scraps
you find or rummage in the street,
recollecting these neglected,
the tiniest leavings—bits of stone,
bits of metal, glass, and wood.
And topplingly you pile up your solemn
statuary. They stand there waiting,
each two-inch child alone in space,
hundreds and hundreds, a millennium
of foundlings in a falling world,

you down there
barely breathing in Brooklyn,

buried live and flinging up
your daily bucket.
The coprophages of success
in the poses of pride, corruption, and wrath
caper on the earth.
You grope in darkness, they grovel in light.

WAKING WORDS

The evening sleeps that stars
may be conceived—see,
they shine, the infant worlds!
How simple that was,
to sleep to the naming
of stars! You slept,
and speech was born in light,
the infant words,
how simple then was!

Come, says happiness,
that anachronism, naming
you and taking your hand
to follow to its early
country. What pleasure now
to see yourself by glow
and fulguration, to be
the star that is here
and star that is there,
the leap and light
—dawn, transparent star!

From LEAPING CLEAR

(1976)

THE HANDBALL PLAYERS AT BRIGHTON BEACH

To David Ritz

And then the blue world daring onward
discovers them, the indigenes, aging,
oiled, and bronzing sons of immigrants,
the handball players of the new world
on Brooklyn's bright eroding shore
who yawp, who quarrel, who shove,
who shout themselves hoarse, don't
get out of the way, grab for odds,
hustle a handicap, all crust,
all bluster, all con and gusto all
on show, tumultuous, blaring,
grunting as they lunge. True,
their manners lack grandeur, and
yes, elsewhere under the sun legs
are less bowed, bellies are less
potted, pates less bald or blanched,
backs less burned, less hairy.

                       So?

So what! the sun does not snub,
does not overlook them, shines,

and the fair day flares,
the blue universe booms and blooms,

the sea-space, the summer high, focuses
its great unclouded scope in ecstatic
perspection—and you see it too
at the edge of the crowd, edge of the sea,
between multitudes and immensity:
from gray cement ball courts under
the borough's sycamores' golden boughs,
against the odds in pure speculation
Brighton's handball heroes leap up half
a step toward heaven in burgundy, blue,
or buttercup bathing trunks, in black
sneakers still stylish after forty years,
in pigskin gloves buckled at the wrist,
to keep the ball alive, the sun up,
the eye open, the air ardent,
festive, clear, crowded with delight.

WAS. WEASEL. ISN'T. IS

WAS

Was dark things bleeding away beyond
their outlines, was walls roaring, closing in,
or subsiding in bruised unaccountable
oblivions. Suddenly, the lights came on:
growing, he was learning, was learning that
bodies and things at ease in their auras
must not be touched until they consent,
can not touch until you say they can.

And everywhere the sun, the early light.
And they, with large features, with large limbs,
benevolent giants in bright colors
on the streets of Brooklyn, moving always
in relation, by courtesy and pleasure,
separate, with a glowing separation,

defined and with a glance of recognition
courting the other's sunlit advancing
definition, the other's passing wish.
Me first! deferred to *After you!*
—with a tip of the hat or a nod
or an arm waving one gallantly on.
There was nothing their enormous bodies,
their gentle manners had not simplified.
Here and there, around a subtle, a consen-
suous point, their purposes, their speeding
maneuvers and high heady murmurs met
and turned in a dance, a steady pacing:
their salutations smile, *Dear Sir Madam Child!*
their partings are signed with open gestures,
Sincerely Truly Cordially yours.
Distance itself consented, itself was touch.
A constellation swarming in the sun
in a common, a communing vibration.

And drifting at night, going to sleep,
he wished with what little of his will
was left, no longer to uphold
the gravity of everything. He said
they could, and saw them fall and flow
together, droplets with little lights
starlike, drinking one another mouth
to mouth, conjoining and clarified.
Under the coiling fluency, on the stones:
the body of transparence lying still.
Eyes open, lips to its boundlessness,
he saw this too, he saw it through and through.

WEASEL

Later, something else: sense
of secrets, choice, couplings, bias,
a broken consensus; sudden
nodes and surging, flares
over a field of crevasses.
Yearning incomplete tender

excited implicated in
the murder of communal majesty
reckless desperate pronged—he feel-
eeleels.
　　　Blackout.
And reappears: triumph
of skepticism in the guise of sex
—or the other way around—
a weasel in a wolfskin, appetite
probing forward, anguish biting back;
acrid awl-toothed ferrets, first
profaning mammal, his notions run
among the old identities,
grand immobile eggs of great saurians,
stave them in with a paw,
dabble sharp noses in the golden yolk
after the hidden copula, the payoff,
tit-for-tat, gobbet of muck on the palm.
What the hell is it all for?
run fast
consume and void
shake a paw at the shit.
Sudden turning, quick shying
of his snout in revulsion.
Despair composed this snob?
Airs blown
from distant bodies.
Digging down, flings dirt backward.
For great cravings small gravings.
And a muddy mouthful.
Screw my fellow man,
my putz is my brother!
Shame shunts him off.
Cross to the other side of the street.
Cover your tracks, move on.
Bestrides the ruined positions.
To live this caricature?
To *live* it.
Prong stiff into the March wind.

ISN'T

Except for reassembled curiosities,
inarticulate vast bone-stacks visited
by dank schoolchildren in dull museums
(half gawk, the others scrawl initials),
or thunder walking upstate in a low
rainless sky over miserable hamlets
where the dead cars brooding in dooryards
outnumber the starving inbred villagers,
scarcely anything survives from that epoch.

IS

Things as they are.
The even voice
weighs them together and says,
Such *and* such, on *both* hands,
see, clod here and *here* cloud,
as they happen to be,
their tactful balance.

The clod in the hand is heavy,
damp, dumb, grainy, old, cold, odd,
composite, shapeless, neutral, small,
sifted through the cleansing worm.
Well, so be it.
                    And so be it.
The sun comes over the cloud,
cloud comes over the clod
—the light, the light-of-hand—
and grass comes up,
singulars out of the earth
lifting their spears and shouting *Ahhhh!*

STANZAS: THE MASTER'S VOICE

Piddling small derivations with large
enthusiasm, taking his puddles for seas,
paddling in a sea of stimuli, to which,
playfully, he over-responded:
imagining perils and then the wave
that lifted him to safety while he struck
vainly at its steep and frightening flank,
then tumbled down bump on the waiting shore.
These were the pleasures of his setting out.

Of his arrival the pleasure was the sounds:
whistles, piping, voices, tall hooting in
the trees, among empty places, out
of high rocks uplifted like organ pipes,
clear calls in wells and holes and hollows and halls.
The world had voices, or was itself a voice,
a garrulous race that spoke all at once,
at random and loudly to no one he could see.

What did manners bid him do? Stay silent,
as one too young, as one not spoken to?
Or greet these breathings with his own replies?
He did them both, soundlessly opening his mouth
in tune and time to the calls that sang about,
that rang more faintly now with his grimacing.
And now beneath he heard the constant scratching sound,

like claws that scrabbled habitations in the stone.
That crackled in his ear as well—his own desire.
Silence then—and then a peeping repeated, like
a small occasional star, was all of sound grown pure.
To father voices, become my father! he swore.
Death had given him a master and vocation.

How easily his competence exceeds the song!
What the master could do once only and then
arduously, he achieves over and over

on the ample pages of his copybook.
He need not strive to compose. Does not. He writes.

The words enclose their own intention.
His art is writing, pure and simple.
He is the completed world's unfailing scribe.
What he writes repeatedly is simply perfection.

Diligence and stillness and peace, his lowered head
and pursed lips, are the little pastime of a large
distraction—he is listening to something else.

From the black shore behind the words, a small child,
a last master, is saying something he can't quite hear.

There is no time, this line has not been written.

BEETHOVEN'S BUST

To Richard Howard

The zero year, the dark eel body,
rushes forward, pours over itself
and disappears under the sky's black rock.
Suburban streets and rain in Buffalo
this Thursday night in harsh November.
City an instant above its falls.
The torrent smashes the lip and thunders
into a brief abyss; hither each guest,
trapped by his mediocre buoyancy,
floats on the swift affluence of conceit,
the sweet influence of wine and chatter,
of laughter, food, electric light.
And music now, a phonograph floods
the scene, a warming clatter of song
includes and moves whatever moves within

—and lends these particles a seemly
magnitude, these dissonants a structure;
so music rehears and rehearses, recalls
and recalls the irrevocable until
what cannot be revoked can almost be
desired, and the dumb fact is fate speaking.

In dry sufficient middle age
they come to on this nether shore,
gathered in bright rooms to toast
a *quartetto* on tour, four famous fiddlers
in turtlenecks and tuxes
who, beaming after Beethoven,
paddle the flux and artfully
snack up compliments like ducks.
Now Fortune wakes, now sits up
and rubs her eyes, presides
at the world's first levee.
These happy few, and if fewer
happier, are happy too to feel
their *angoisse provinciale* warming
to provincial self-complacence.
Glances are exchanged:
the continents and capitals
drift into range.
Passwords pass:
the universe is middle-class.
Whoever piqued themselves on making do
with second best, discover now they do not
know one another, have never met, maneuver
by delicate mutual repulsions,
veering to avoid the other's wake as if
it were a wine of desuetude that could make
them ponderous, bristling, and obsolete
—battleships among the swans.
                                        Indeed,
they strive to see beyond each other, vie
to see beyond each other's seeing, beyond
even the visiting stars, into

a place never seen, too transparent to be
a place, timeless, too bright. As far
as any eye can see all outside is
a belated guest running for the door,
then nothing more, the dark incivility,
the rain, more darkness, nothing more.

                                      Meanwhile,
the successes perfect their extraversion;
their glance when they look at others is bold
and gleams with pleasure and incredulity
—"What, you here? you lucky stiff!"

Whatever his luck, he too is here,
in from the rain to blunder for comfort,
the pleasure of standing in a crowd,
has brought his antique precocity,
his style the changeling prince—unknown
to himself and yet suspecting greatness—
his air startled, indignant, sniffish,
as if he'd caught the devil cheating at cards
or, simply, defecating on the deck.

Somebody's poet, he is introduced
to somebody's mother. It is poetry
they speak of, not motherhood,
though not at first, for first she recalls
her history, Junker girlhood, husband
—precocious martyr—murdered in a camp
in the thirties; then half casually,
almost a throwaway, "He was not even
a Jew. *Ach,* go read about it
in Shirer, if you like!"—gratuitous
infidelity from which she has not
recovered, will not, forty years after,
forgive.
          Recalling the irrevocable?
Well, music of a sort, someone gagging
on a spine. *This* horror doesn't go down
for all her swallowing, won't come up
for all her saying it out.

And has *he,*
he wonders, been accused, impertinent Jew
who didn't die? He almost hears the slap,
death repeating its insult on her face,
sees the face stunned white with failure
before it stings red with shame.
So it is better to speak of poetry
—their theme, aptly, Death and the maiden—
while the dark eavesdropper, the final
husband, sidles closer with the shadows,
a mock martini chilling in his hand.
Hair poked out like stuffing from a dollhead
tatter, face scored and delicate and white
—old shell or shipwrecked moon in daylight—
she calls for silence with yellowed fingers
and searching for words stoops and peers,
lady at the oven door who drags out
piping in their pie after fifty years
the verses of her German youth.

Hölderlin, Rilke, Mörike, Schiller . . .
the names of great dead poets drop.
Oh matinee idols of Eternity,
great brows and noses glimmering to
the farthest rows, the highest balcony,
their oversized Orphic heads now float
along the carpet's lotuses and sing
on death's Parnassus all the endless
artificial noon.
                    Just now, tonight,
they are praising loveliness of women
who know that poetry's a caress,
language purified to sweetnothingness,
showers of seed on a shadowy Eve.
Ruhe, Ruhe, she croons aloud. Remembrance
and reverie, release and rest,
engender in a vowel, *Ruhe, Ruhe:*
lulled, tumescent, gravid with
an endless, gray, and even sea,

its Baltic strand where, royal maiden,
she galloped brown horses in the foam.
And who can save her in the swart sea?
Follow me! follow me! the hooves plash away.
Poor bedeviled prince who cannot rest,
into the sea's little profundity
he whips his marvelous mount, out toward
the water charm, the voices, and the voice
within the voices revealing his name.

Only the swell wrinkling under a wind,
a wake too wide to be a wake,
a world too wide to be the world,
nothing there, no one to save,
no maid, no martyr, no people,
and the prince himself gone far under,
weighed down by armor, waterlogged.
Only a child's kingdom under the wave,
the first light darkening, the faintest babble
from above, a muted sociable flutter
of tunings, teasing, footsteps, puffing
that blows out the candles on the cake,
a fading cheer!—music too awkward
and small, too homely and young to leave
its little orchestra, spoons shovels beds
(domestic murmur and tinkle and tears),
too brief to recall time from other places
or send it spiraling in long eddies.
A crone like a cork bobbing in time!
A generation whirled beyond his senses!
He braces to take it all on his back,
to uphold the flood, if flood is all there is.
Lungs scorched with salt, about to burst,
he sees the silver burble of his cry
gaily ascend the silent deep.
The chain of light fishes him out.

Surfaces and kicks for shore, escapes it all
—with what alacrity! Swallows sweet heavens.

So we are born, in our instant of greatest
terror. The mighty stay long until
they leap screaming for the world; others
patter in as lightly as the rain.
From nameless dying he could not bear,
he is born naming the horror, choking
on the name.
                Dawn.
                        And now
you hear a first intelligent croak
sounding in the littoral grass
—human, almost; suddenly you
imagine the eyes, *if* you can bear it!—
then farther off and going fast, as though
toward its dismal lair, the patter perhaps
of light *faux pas,* then
a little sigh at last.

So, *voilà!* here they are after all,
high and dry in the corner
of a darkened parlor, on a sofa
tilting off toward the end of time,
mediocre muse, poor poet—he
doesn't please, she can't inspire—
cast away from the party together,
almost like maiden and boy
their matchmaking families marooned
and already seem hardly to miss
—while elsewhere in other rooms
the party sorts itself through chances
and changes, deferences and differences,
makes a sense of sorts circling around
its empty center, the dead one, the lost
martyr, the silence riddling the structure.

Let us step back now, as the lamplight
seems to, and permit them, semi-
strangers abashed and silent, to sit
forgotten where time's plunging
has flung them for a moment half-

unaware in puzzled abstraction.
Each, absorbed by his divergent dreaming,
dreams alone, but in our departing view
disposed as if they occurred
on a picture's visionary plane,
neutral, full, abstract, eternal
—she a princess at seventy
shaking off death's importunate arm
around her shoulder, he
a frog of forty
sitting on Beethoven's bust,
trying to understand.

LEAPING CLEAR

Circumambulate the city of a dreamy Sabbath afternoon. Go from Corlears
Hook to Coenties Slip, and from thence, by Whitehall, northward. What do
you see? —*Posted like silent sentinels all around the town, stand thousands*
upon thousands of mortal men fixed in ocean reveries.
—HERMAN MELVILLE

1

Excrescence, excrement, earth
belched in buildings—the city
is the underworld in the world.
They wall space in or drag it down,
lock it underground in holes and subways,
fetid, blackened, choking.
                              Shriveled, small,
grimed with coal and ash, shovel in hand,
his dust-sputting putz in the other,
like death's demiurge come up to look
around, to smudge the evening air,
the old Polack janitor on Clinton Street,
turd squat in the tenement anus,
stands half-underground in darkness
of the cellar steps and propositions

passing children in a broken tongue.
Quickly, they crowd, they age, they plunge
into holes, and are set to work.

   2

Encountered at estuary
end across beaches and dunes,
or opening out of the breakwater's
armlock, a last magnitude
of bay, or beyond the crazywork
of masts and rigging down a street
suddenly, the sea stuns
moving into itself, gray over
green over gray, with salt smell
and harbor smells, tar, flotsam,
fish smell, froth, its sentient
immense transparent space.

Walking in Coney Island, bicycling
in Bay Ridge on the crumbling water-level
promenade under the Verrazano,
walking the heights above the Narrows, driving
on Brooklyn Heights, then slowly at night
under the East River Drive past the empty
fish market, past Battery Park, and then
northward driving along the rotting piers,
or looking downriver from Washington Heights
into the harbor's distant opening,
I recovered one summer in New York
the magical leisure of the lost sea-space.
Breathing, I entered, I became
the open doorway to the empty marvel,
the first Atlantis of light.

Windy sun below the Narrows,
Gravesend scud and whitecaps,
coal garbage gravel
scows bucking off Bensonhurst,

Richmond blueblurred
westward, and high
into the blue
supreme clarity,
it gleams aloft, alert
at the zenith
of leaping, speed
all blown to the wind
—what, standing in air,
what does it say
looking out out out?

And the light
                    (everywhere,
off ridge, rock, window, deep,
drop) says,
                    I leap clear.

    3

Recalled from the labor of creation,
it was glancing as it flew, and saw
looking out to it the shimmering
of the million points of view. To see
Brooklyn so on a sabbath afternoon
from the heights, to be there beyond
the six days, the chronicle of labors,
to stand in the indestructible space,
encompass the world into whose center
you fly, and be the light looking!

The demiurge of an age of bronze
sees his handiwork and says it is good,
laying down his tools forever.
To see Brooklyn so in the spacious ease
of sabbath afternoon above the Narrows
is to say over and over what our speechless eyes
behold, that it is good, it is good, the first
Brooklyn of the senses, ardent and complete
as it was in the setting out of the sabbath.

AN ERA OF LAUGHTER

At the onset of an era of laughter, it was thought to restore the integrity of the temple with satire. How proficient everyone became (and how delighted to discover this universal talent)! Even the dullest were soon masters of ridicule and could satirize satire itself, while the few who could not grew expert in the modes of laughter. There was nothing but laughter—laughter and integrity.

When the blind dwarf (manacled, unkempt) was led in, the temple, as if not to be outdone, tittered and roared, cast itself down and rolled on the ground in a devastating parody of collapse. Nor were they spared who kept aloof—you, for example, who read this text smirking amid smithereens. Private smiles blend nicely enough into the general shambles of idiocy.

THE PRODIGAL

Fifty years and not a nickel to his name,
the fat lines of his credit expunged,
his heritage the milt-clouded muck,
he dreams he is a victim, dog-bitten,
flea-chancred—The Disinherited One
he calls himself, plunking down three last words.
And so he runs with the runts and weird,
the world's culls and thwarts, a desert wrath
slavering for the succulent towns.
His cohort, his conquering dolts, crowds
an outlying village street. *We have
come back!* they shout, but their joyous
mutilated cries summon no faces
to the horrified windows, bring salt
foaming out of the broken roadways.
Dire under the stars, they know it now:
earth detests them. They buzz about

in confusion, dismay, terror, rubbing
their snub noses over long stupid cheeks
and turn their simple sullen faces
here and there, casting for a way back
into the wilderness—the founding fathers
of the second republic.

WHO'S WHO (AND WHAT'S WHAT)

Nervous and vital, he, too, danced forward to heave his
flaming javelin at the band of elders who barred his way to the
secret and the treasure. And yet, although he clamored and
raged in the forefront, the attackers were so many, he found
himself too far off to tell if he had dented that fussy reticence
and dull certitude, that infuriating self-complacence. And if
now and again one of them fell, it seemed, filtered through that
distance, the result of invisible blows.

But when, long after, he had struggled to the top of the little
eminence where they stood, his sword out to skewer the old
bastards once and for all, they said, spreading their arms (and
neither weakness nor fear could perturb their sluggish
pentameters),

We thought you'd never reach us with relief,
you've been so long. Now come and stand where we
have stood, hold up the standard we've upheld!

Their standard (as he saw for the first time) of shame (as he
thought almost for the last) was a bit of bloodied bedsheet, the
elders feeble beyond belief, and their secret, their treasure, there
below them on the plain, a city of graves. Now he understood
they were in fact death's brightest, bravest face, turned not to
guard but to hide—with overweening pity or else in shame
they could offer no better—their horrid town from the eyes of
the thronging young.

No longer a will and its blindness but a fatality and its
intelligence (such as it was)—and no less embattled than he'd

always been—he, too, with a senile passion for repetition, tirelessly joined in the carping antiphon, barking out his odious part at the horde pressing toward them,

Stay where you are!
                    So it has always been.
So must it always be.
                    I told you so.

PHILOSOPHY AND THE TRAP

Trying to think yourself backward out of is how you discover philosophy—in the trap. Naturally, you suppose blindly living forward got you into it, the trap. In this, like the fox—who gnaws his foot, having come to believe (reasonably, since its pain attacks him) his foot is the trap.

Things cannot be so simple for you. Backtracking, you fit your three into the four that first came your way. Always out of time, your escape from *this* trap is, over the long run, to devour yourself completely—and you are to be last inferred daintily stalking the dayspring on four phantom feet.

Once out, once free, you comprehend that as the air comprehends this. Life takes the bait, thought incorporates the trap.

THE GIFT

From the first, the gods were strangers who came among them, observing but keeping their distance, not sitting around the fire exchanging morsels or anecdotes of the road, not mingling under the blankets or quite meeting their eyes in the morning.

156

Gradually, therefore, they sought to catch their eye, to be acknowledged, finally, at all costs, to seduce the gods. The violence of their gestures in the dance, of their shadows around the fire, of their copulations could not compel the interest of the gods who appeared to desire neither their triumphs nor their sacrifices, not their success in the hunt or their most fruitful delvings or the signs and objects by which they thought to assure these.

They came at last to ignore the gods, then to forget them, and went about their affairs as before, although now each thing seemed united with indifference, seemed to possess a neutrality, a final clarity that could have come, as they had already forgotten, only from the gods.

ANTONIO, *BOTONES*

Para Aguirre

Tourist, traveler, consider this child:
Antonio, *botones* * of the Ida Hotel,
of every hierarchy the base,
the bottom of every heap. Oh too clearly
one sees it: vainly God flexes and waxes
His most apparent effulgence, wanly
He wanes in the lens of the soul of
Antonio the dull, the unperceiving.
And a little lower only, the Caudillo
(who dreams he is a boy pillaging apples)
has thrown an aged leg on the high hedge
of heaven and tottering atop the backs
of his Ministries (not excluding *Hacienda,*
not forgetting *Información y Turismo*)
tries to hoist himself up and clamber over.
Push, push, push me higher! his order flies

* Spanish: bellboy.

down from the apex of effort, along the chain
of command, by way of the Ida's owner,
its "maiter dee," desk clerk, barman, straight down
to Antonio in the lobby. And there
the little bell is pinging wildly, Oh please,
Antonio, for the love of heaven, just
a tiny bit higher!
                    And he on whom so much
depends, his jacket spattered, one button
dangling, ears clotted with cotton, his eyes
glazing, his nose just about to be picked,
Antonio the absentminded, the empty-headed,
sleeps on his feet, hears nothing, fails to grab
this client's valise, to open the outer door,
or pick up an unspeakable butt
disgracing the lobby and the noble carpet
—and witless, unwitting, spares the Caudillo
ultimate vulgarity: success in heaven.

Lowest of the low, Antonio, *botones*
of the Ida Hotel (two stars twinkle
on its lintel), Antonio, lowlier still
than the hem of the little chambermaid's skirt:
he's like earth and like the feet of turtles
—he bears all slowly, himself stays hidden.
The traffic flow of orders down the pure,
the crystalline pyramid terminates here
in a puddle, a cipher, a fourteen-year-old failure.
Others glimpse the summit, hear a faint cacophony,
the Leader's stertorous cries, and they respond,
they go higher, come closer, see clearer—but not he.
Then who will clean the lens of Antonio's soul,
so smutted and smutched, so foggy and gray?
Not the Caudillo and his ministers; not
the technocrats, their meager darlings; or
the middle-class poets of Mao who chant
the pompless despots of the magic capitals;
not the saints in their cells, or cadres in theirs.
True, each one wants Antonio for his army

(maybe he's a muse? he seems to inspire them all,
for his sake they pray, profess, or rule—they say)
—but something in this world has to be gray.
Then let it be the soul of Antonio,
unsalvageably so!
                    See,
wipe the slate clean, the slate stays gray!
—and makes the more brilliant those brilliancies
that great men scrawl . . . all over Antonio, who else?
. . . before they pass on (and, naturally, don't think
to tip). Never mind! humble beneath humility,
he asks for nothing—it makes the ages weep.
Never mind! so faint, so fine the line between
acceptance of everything and consent
to injustice, the saints, the very saints
in bliss, even San Anónimo in his,
eyes blinded with their souls' radiance,
drag chains across it continually.
Never mind!
—Shall shade shine, or earth be lustrous?
—Oh surely not until the fiery blast
of God's breath pronounces final judgment!
But brilliance justifies itself, you say, and I
agree, I agree to all this glory
                                   —and yet,
tourist, traveler, set down your suitcase here awhile,
consider Antonio, how his father comes
and beats him, how he takes his money, how
the Caudillo, impaled on the hedge of heaven,
cries aloud in his agony, If only
this innocent would try a little harder!
and urges him on for the glory of Spain
and its rightful place in the Common Market
—useless, of course, but what can you do?—
and how his boss, fed up to here, throws him out
and two days later can't remember his name
—while prancing ably in his place you note
his junior *confrère,* the former incumbent of
the Suiza y Niza (one star) down the street.

Consider Antonio, this simpleton,
this put-upon unresentful child, who can't smell
the carrot (yet feels the stick), who elicits
your sympathy as he thwarts your interest,
who tempts you to tamper with injustice
—only to drop your luggage on your feet:
                                    cram
your pride of life in his lens, see the world
as he must see it—then your eyes are stiffed,
then spasm cramps your brains, then effulgence
stains and shining shames and brilliance blemishes.
—Oh impossible to live there, awful to visit!
Nothing to do but take off on a trip
—and leave Antonio, incorrigibly
unpathetic, unorganizable as dirt,
creatively screwing up still another job.

But who is this leaping for your valise?
Well, it's not the local clod, it's not
Antonio, thank God! What a relief! someone
a centimeter taller, some blue-eyed go-getter,
leaps from the desk, leaps for the door, his buttons
blinking out your warmest welcome, Francisco
by name. Now here's a boy who doesn't appall
the clientele or his bosses. Efficiency's
transparency, looking at is seeing through;
it's like the swallowing of a good gullet;
no glum opacity, no crap in your craw,
nothing retrograde: indeed, the future
personified beside a revolving door.
One sees beyond him to the world as one
has always wished to see it—sunny Mallorca!
under the international sun, white furnace
of a furious polyglot declaring
in simultaneous Swedish, English, French:
I too am a tourist rushing here and there,
although, truthfully, nothing new is under me,
a man of my time until I'm pensioned off
and relocated semi-permanently

—among damp shadows of the cheaper season
on a tideless island, with no tongue of my own.

August 1974

THE SECRET WORK

Nadezhda Mandelstam has told the story. In Strunino, after her husband's arrest, working the night shift in a textile factory, she runs, sleepless and distraught, among the machines, chanting his forbidden poems to herself to preserve them. And so for twenty-five years in Perm, in Moscow, in Voronezh, Leningrand, Ulyanovsk, Samatikha . . .

A man with chills hugs himself,
rejoicing in his fever. She,
the frozen century's daughter, rejoices
in her secret, hugs to herself
the prophet hiding in her breath,
the infant she keeps close, safe, swaddled,
speaking.
              She covers over, makes him
smaller, safer, no bigger than
a seed, a spark—search where they will,
they will not find him here, yet here
he is, a little voice praying,
an enormous voice prophesying,
this live coal held on her tongue
burning behind clenched teeth.

To herself, in herself, over
and over, what must not
be said aloud, not written down,
not whispered in corners or left
to be smelled out clotting
at the ends of broken phrases
 . . . the poems of Mandelstam
going out in Siberia's night.

EGG

1

Not
this mind,
these puns, a periplus
around a cosmion,
not mind widening this egg
to whiteness, a
universal, an o-
void in an omega, mind's
timeless waste:
poor
farm
pure
form;
not its dance of staggers, lame
capering caliper tacking
pegleg to legleg,
a moving mutiny around
a mute unity

that curves from salience
to silence, minding the store
with round redounding, O
mumly peepless!
its white the neutralest
effulgence;
             no, not
mind, blind in the blank,
feeling a way by longings,
shortcomings, listing at large
a topography of stumble,
ego type-tapping, *Eggo*
eggo echo eccomi!
replicating aspects of egg
as ectoplasm, a ghostly
difference,
             while going

about egg's beaued belly, belled
back—O, mothering curve
of contemplation!—mind
muttering, mumming;
                    not
this oaf of I'lls and ills, pale
aleph, cipher, white blighter
on its dancing chip over the dark
deep: not this mind in terror
of time, bringing its white treasure
on the wild tangents, yawing farther
into itself, its lurid, its phantom
sea;
      not this, not
these.

       2

O
-word, the
bird's cry, the o-
vum comes
in a cluck, in a clackle
of slime and lime:
this
egg
is
fresh,
minty and sage,
a wight right in greenward weeds
beside the green sea
at dawn,
this egg is all
for the day's throne,
the sun's slide up the sky.
Inside, a joke, a son
in a see, an I
in an eye in an *Ei:* these puns
are fatal are

fertile,
duplicating with a difference
a various redundancy,
the gold conflagrance
that differs into a dupling heart,
an oeufre,
orf Lèvre of or-feathers
-fingers -feeders -features -fecker!
An incubus.
An imp-unity.

Time crows over the crackling and over
the rising sun. The difference lives!
The chickling cheeps, I am the difference!

3

Madam, Sir, abashed and saddened before
your own, your particular fates
—to differ, double, die:
Smile, idiots, look
at the birdie!

THE THIEF OF POETRY

1

Girls he took from friends at seventeen
he lost in months and never found again.
Not so the books he stole that year:
face à face with his pounding heart
a *Fleurs du mal* translated to fact
under the null persona of his coat,
and closer still, like a blade slipped
through the dark intercostal spaces,
Eliot's *Poems* spirited from Macy's
in a folded X-ray of his lungs.

When he read "Prufrock" in the subway home
that afternoon, he was a cat crouched
before a saucer of milk: nothing moved
in all that train that illicit hour
but the pink tip of his tongue
and the white pages turning.

2

He waited all that year where three
roads meet—love, art, thievery—
in a wilderness of rumbling stone
while the great caravans went by
surging with goods and grief, waited
for lightning to point the way.
Lightning struck.
Was it defect of intelligence
or excessive timidity, a curse
that made vapid the family seed,
or simply an instant's inattention,
the tiniest mothhole bitten clear
through the universe? what made him take
words for the lightning that lit them,
bowls of milk for ah! bright breasts?

3 *Oedipus or Sophocles: The Road Not Taken*

He has been telling it with a sigh
—for sure!—ages and ages since.
Who might have gone limping toward Thebes
came prattling to Athens.

THE CITY AND ITS OWN

Among the absolute graffiti which
—stenciled, stark, ambiguous—command
from empty walls and vacant lots,
POST NO BILLS, NO TRESPASSING HERE:
age and youth—Diogenes, say,
and Alexander, dog-philosophy
and half-divine, too-human imperium—
colliding, linger to exchange ideas
about proprietorship of the turf.
Hey, mister, you don't own the sidewalk!
Oh yeah?
Yeah! the *city* owns the sidewalk—*mister!*
Oh yeah! says *who?*
Thus power's rude *ad hominem* walks all over
the civil reasoner, the civic reason.

Everyone has something.
Everything is someone's.

The city is the realm of selves in rut
and delirium of ownership, is property,
objects made marvelous by prohibition
whereby mere things of earth become ideas,
thinkable beings in a thought-of world
possessed by men themselves possessed by gods.

So I understood at twelve and thirteen,
among the throngs of Manhattan,
that I dodged within a crowd of gods
on the streets of what might be heaven.
And streets, stores, stairs, squares, all
that glory of forbidden goods, pantheon
of properties open to the air,
gave poor boys lots to think about!
And then splendor of tall walkers
striding wide ways, aloof and thoughtful
in their nimbuses of occupation,

advancing with bright assurance as if
setting foot to say, *This is mine, I
am it*—and passing on to add,
now yield it to you, it is there.
Powers in self-possession, their thinking
themselves was a whirling as they went,
progressing beyond my vista to possess
unthought-of worlds, the wilderness.

These definitions, too, have meant to draw
a line around, to post and so prohibit,
and make our vacant lot a sacred ground.
Here then I civilize an empty page
with lines and letters, streets and citizens,
making its space a place of marvels now
seized and possessed in thought alone.
You *may* gaze in, you *must* walk around.
—Aha (you say), conceit stakes out its clay!
—*That* is a cynic's interpretation,
pulling the ground out from under my feet;
I fall, I fear, within your definition
which, rising and dusting off my knees,
civilly I here proclaim our real estate,
ours in common, the common ground
of self, a mud maddened to marvel
and mingle, generously, in generation.

A PLAYER'S NOTES

To Hashim Khan

1 There is impatience in many disguises—weariness, reluctance, zeal, the
desire to win, the fear of losing.

2 What is not impatience is the game, pure and simple.

3 Properly presented, with patient attentiveness, the ball is a surprise his opponent would not wish to refuse, will, with appropriate care, wish to return in kind.

4 Failing to attend to his opponent, he is doomed to try to exceed himself, is doomed further to succeed in defeating himself.

5 Playing for self-transcendence, he wastes and destroys himself, lags behind in order to fly forward too fast at the last instant.

6 Always the phoenix, unhappy bird who appears only on the threshold of the calcined house.

7 The game is not intended to flourish on the wreckage of reality.

8 Truly, reluctance (weariness, failure to attend) causes him to arrive late for the ball. Just as truly, his desire to fly, his dream that he can fly, that he is flying, cause him to arrive late for the ball.

9 The daydream of flight spreads its phantom pinions in the lost instant of his failure to attend.

10 Dropped onto the treadmill of his daydream, one ball will never reach him, while the other in the freedom of the game rushes past with a savage whirring of wings.

11 Gasping for breath, he asks, Is it possible to survive here without being reborn?

12 Rebirth—if that is the issue—comes from renewed contact with the eternal, as in its momentary flight on the court.

Therefore, these are forbidden, these are enjoined.

13 Forbidden: hairsplitting, pessimism, fantasy.

14 Enjoined: knowledge, good humor, the exchanging of gifts.

A TALE OF A NEEDLER AND A NAILER

When everyone was going out
to brilliant day, to vivid night,
something had to be given up,
years ago when the world began,
something had to be left behind:
a token to darkness
a prize to the past
a nod to night
a nickel to mortality at the gate.
Let it be me! they said,
me, me, *I'll* stay.
I sew the world to sleep!
I hammer the world awake!

Who *were* they? you ask.
The tiniest old men
who never were born,
twins, in fact,
and bent together
like halves of an O
but back to back,
a thousand years they'd need
just to straighten up
—what stubbornness, such loyalty
to the shape of a room!
And such doom
—like two little children
trapped in old age,
who can't grow up, who can't grow back.
A nailer, a tailor,
the one and the other.

And here today, right now,
at the top of the stairs,
with bent-up nail
and beat-up chair
on a broken floor
with a hammer only

and all of his might,
the nailer hammers, he hums
aloud to himself,

"Hey, watch out,
stand back there,
don't crowd me!
Dummy, can't you see?
this hammer's no toy,
the thing itself!
a hammer for real,
wood handle, iron head,
just see it flash
its sky's-worth of arc,
it drives home
in a single blow!
—the whole of heaven
on the head of a nail.

"Now who would have thought
you could get so much
on the head of a nail?
A nail? a nail? who said a nail?
Children, did *I* say a nail?
Now you've got my goat.
I don't *need* a nail.
See, I throw it out
and I hammer away."

True, true, he hammers away.

And back to his back,
his brother stoops,
too patient, too still
to stitch in time,
with one little needle
and one bit of thread
and one ray of light
where dust specks blaze,
where filaments float:

"Cloth is waiting,
the button waits.
I squeeze my eye
to needle's eye.
By smaller degrees
and more and more quietly
and last so you can't even see,
I bring the thread near."

Then they glow in the trap
and they answer each other:
I pound the world apart.
I sew the world to stay.
Here's a knap on your noodle.
Here's thread in your eye.
I speak louder.
But *I've* the last say.

Bang! says one.
Shhh, says the other.

THE GOLDEN SCHLEMIEL

So there's a cabbie in Cairo named Deif.
So he found 5000 bucks in the back seat.
So meanwhile his daughter was very sick.
So he needed the money for medicine bad.
So never mind.
So he looked for the fare and gave it back.
So then the kid died.
So they fired him for doing good deeds on company time.
So the President heard it on the radio.
So he gave him a locally built Fiat.
So I read it in the papers.
So you read it here.

A poor man has less than weight, has negative gravity, his life a
  slow explosion. Barely he makes the days meet. Like doors
  they burst open. Money, job, daughter fly away from him.
  Irony, injustice, bits of horror come close, cohere.

They are with us, the poor, like the inner life which is wantless
  too; our souls' white globes float somehow in the blue,
  levitating and bobbing gently at middle height over the
  bubbling fleshpots.

Our effort to remake the found world as the lost reverie is
  desire.

So, little Yasmin was sick, sick to the point of dying.
She was like a garden coughing and drying.
And suddenly her salvation was there, a sheepskin, yes,
a satchel of money meekly baaing from the rear.
A miracle in the offing?
That famous retired philanthropist named God
was back in business? was starting to take a hand?
directing things maybe from the back seat?
Maybe.

Restored to its rich owner (he tipped a fig and a fart, a
  raspberry of plump nil), lying safely on his lap, the money
  was mute again, was superfluity, and root and sum and
  symbol, both lettuce and lump, of all evil.
She too approaching that state,
Yasmin, a flower, meantime, dying.

For the locally assembled daughter a locally assembled Fiat.

Too wantless to imagine the money his?
Spurned the miracle and thwarted the grace?
So loved the law he gave it his only begotten daughter?
Effed and offed his own kid?
Saint and monster, poor man and fool,
slowly exploding, Deif all this.
Yes, one melts at his meekness,
scoffs at the folly, trembles

for his stupor of bliss of obedience,
gasps at his pride, weeps
for his wantlessness,
grunts when irony that twists the mouth jabs the gut.
Then horror—the dark miracle—roaring, leaps
into the front seat, grabs the wheel and runs you down in the
    street
—while you sit on a café terrace innocently reading the paper
or, bent above a radio, feel the news waves break against your
    teeth.

Deif in grief. Deif in mourning. Deif bereaved.
Deif in the driver's seat. Deif without a beef.

And daily in four editions and every hour on
the hour, the media heap your dish with images
of sorrows and suffering, cruelty, maiming, death.
(Our real griefs in their imaginary jargons.)
And you cannot touch a single sufferer, comfort
one victim, or stay any murderous hand.
Consumer of woes, the news confirms you
in guilt, your guilt becomes complicity,
your complicity paralysis, paralysis
your guilt; elsewhere always, your life becomes
an alibi, your best innocence a shrug,
your shrug an unacknowledged rage, your rage
is for reality, nothing less. Yes,
you feel, murder would be better than hanging around;
if only your fist could penetrate the print,
you too might enter the reality of news. . . .
You switch the radio on, hungrily turn the page
of sorrows and suffering, cruelty, maiming, death.

Pasha, President, playboy swing masterfully
above our heads—what style! what heroes!—fling themselves
over the headlines into the empyrean
beyond our lowly weather—ah, *there* all the news
is blue and blank, those soarings, those mock descents,
they are writing their own tickets in heaven.
Fortune, true, is spiteful and fickle, and glamour

itself must stalk them—but cannot shoot so high
as impotence dreams, as resentment wishes.
Gorgeous, limber, and free, like our consciences,
a law unto themselves, a darker law to us
—in their suntans our shadow.

And where they fly, the lines of force accompany,
the patterns of deference continue to comfort,
a maggotism distracting irony.
Their rods flatten others, their staffs flatter *them*
—you and I pay for the lies we get,
but heroes get the lies they pay for.
So here's the President's ear on the radio's belly
—if there are rumbles in Egypt, he'll know it,
he'll proclaim, Fix this! (*Fixed!*), Do this! (*Done!*).
And here is Deif's story beating at his eardrum.
Tremble, mock, shrug, or writhe, you and I
cannot write the ending, cannot snatch glory
of authorship from anonymity of events.
The President can. The President does.
His literature is lives, is Deif smiling:
golden, seraphic and sappy, sheepish, sweet;
is Deif not understanding a thing and grateful
and happy like a puppy given to a child.
He speaks: his fiat is a Fiat,
assembled locally and worth five grand
(out of the President's pocket? Pal, guess again!)
—which cancels Deif's deed down to the penny.
Deif has no claim on the moral law, no dignity,
no destiny, no daughter; his suffering
won't embarrass, his monstrousness appall;
injustice is removed, and nothing left in its place,
the spot swept clear, blood expunged, crowd dispersed,
and Deif himself sent to park around the corner,
a bystander to his life, a pure schlemiel.
Deif never did anything, nothing ever happened
—all for the greater glory of the State.

Exit Deif with his dead daughter in his arms.
Re-enter Deif in a Fiat meekly beeping,

and overhead, Yasmin, the locally dis-
assembled, the wingèd, pointing down and proudly beaming.

Upon such sacrifices the gods themselves shy clods.

Riffling the pages of sorrow and suffering,
the President carefully lowers his hydrocephalic head onto
    the news he made.

Besides, the State abhors the inner life, finds its rich
    wantlessness, its invisible reverie uninteresting because
    unmanageable, damned because unusable. Incapable of
    inactivity, the State cannot submit to stillness and seeks
    precisely to create the desire it will manage. It requires
    neither pensive persons nor upright citizens but a smiling
    multitude. The State is a Midas. Every absence and
    invisibility it would make bright material, for what is
    invisible—Deif's resolve to return the money or patient grief
    recollecting the spilt petals of his lost jasmine—what is
    invisible the State believes deplorable, knows to be
    dangerous. Such is the anxiety that caused the President to
    lift a finger, to touch Deif.

To reconstitute the found Fiat as the lost daughter.

Wheeled, powerful, in progress; altar and throne
and golden veal, leviathan and juggernaut;
and nearby, one Reda Deif—once slowly
exploding, once a spirit darkening
all earthly glory—observes the State
adoring itself as its image.

Easy to amend injustice. Hard to be just.

Deif attending the vehicle.
His *air de chauffeur,* a man
who defers to a car, infers
his value from his deference.
He bows, approaching the door,
bows to the aura and glory
around, behind, beyond, within

this scrap of State, this scrim
of status before the reeling stars;
he bows to be bowing. Air
now of one waiting for
its owner to appear. Deif knows
it can't be Deif, must be another:
grand, glowing, ponderous, a meteor,
breathtaker and heartstealer, mover and shaker,
who merely presuming possesses,
imposes, distresses between his flashing
attraction, his haughty don't-touch!
Let poorman-Deif dare show his face,
guarddog-Deif will show him the door!
He shifts from foot to foot
beside himself beside the car.
Embarrassment? Well,
ecstasy.

Seepage of eternity we call the sea, the sky.
Such spacious summer nights come also to Deif,
the sky enormous, intimate, Deif too brief, too dusky.
The universe invites him to fly—if only he *could* fly!
It snatches his heart and throws it into the blue.
The cosmic wafting blows it away.
Must I? Must I follow?
he asks the whirlwind's roar.
His heart will shatter to encompass all
or, lightless coal, plummet through the dark and azure!
Lies down again, throbbing, where he was. Schlemiel
and saint and monster are cradled and tucked in.

However theatrically laid on thick by fate, how did this tiny
   whisper of injustice exceed the general and deafening static of
   woe?
Do you think Deif's boss called a press conference to announce
   the shafting?
Or that his neighbors issued a news release?
Do you think Deif himself told the story?
Really? him? that schlemiel? And to whom in that Calcutta on
   the Nile?

Maybe you think it doesn't flatter the President a little too
    neatly?
Think it isn't the least bit imaginary?
No poets of Presidency in Egypt?
No P.R. men in Cairo?
Do you think there really is a man named Deif?

I think I prefer to think that Deif exists,
yes, and even little Yasmin dead dead dead
indeed, dead for a fact.
I think I prefer this horror
which tells me it is possible to feel
if not to believe.
Only horror survives our raging irony
and we survive by horror.

So one delves a death and turns . . . a pretty penny,
some moral quid for all that mortal quo (O wit
for woe!)—O "think" and "feel," increments
of spirit that transfuse, that elevate! Erect
atop her grave, and now a great heart gushes, floods
the frame with gladdening news: One *has* come through!
—which makes one, after all, complicit, one's spade
a spade, Yasmin, Deif one's victims, one's life
vicarious, vacant, oneself a fiction
held up to a fate, shattered by a fury.
Pluck out your radio, rend your paper!
Savage death demands a savage discipline.
Down your head, roll in the dirt, mourn!

As to bad before, so now to better fortune:
Deif submits. Incorrigible schlemiel,
he doesn't grab it with both hands,
one on each tit. See him!
insulated from the earth by rubber,
two fingers gingerly on the wheel,
his other arm out to catch the breeze
as he drives into the sunset of the real,
his position false but increasingly familiar.
Fortune sits on him like a ton of shit

—a raven of another choler—and smiles.
Sociably, he returns the smile.

Farewell, Deif! Farewell, brother!

THIS WAY TO THE EGRESS

Impatient to be under way, he boarded early; still the boat
delayed at quayside, then floated off into the house of spooks.
What a disappointment that was! Where are the real terrors,
he demanded, for which he'd spent his life preparing? Oh, but
the eulogy of terror—*any* eulogy—would have stultified his
dying, kept him as he was, an aging man becalmed in the
luminous still sea of his transcendence. Instead, these too obvious frights, all burlap and cotton batting and sprung wires,
an old mattress dump, unbelievable!—it wouldn't fool, much
less terrify, a child—and revolting! the stink swaddled his
head, he would have vomited—and then the wine- and urine-
stewed supers who manned its machinery, headsmen and skele-
tons, murderous crones and farting trumps that made a pass at
troubling the dark—couldn't the universe do any better than
that! What a sendoff, who'd *want* to come back! So he kibitzed
his dying, feeling mocked and cheated, it was so unworthy, so
demeaning.

Of course, something kibitzed him back. That was the
ordeal of laughter. (It could have been better.) Storms of hooting and heckling drove him backward, each affronting buffet
pushily took a bit of his life. Swept away, unable not to be
where he'd been before, how much he should have liked to
join in the party, draw power from the chorus of wise guys
and with it howl out the last laugh, be *named* Laughter—mockery's own mascot—and claw his way back to himself, to anywhere! But the laugh machine really *was* laughing—to itself
and yet at him, as if it were his own râling breath, mocking
and sustaining, or this little boat of wires and tubes that bore
him so poorly. Mad, mechanical, unreal, still the laughter

was appropriate and, therefore, genuine, had to possess *some* understanding. He saw that. He *was* ridiculous, not heroic at all, a little boy, and maybe less than that, a baby, probably, who couldn't wipe his own behind. And all his rage a huffing grotesquerie, as if to give death a scare—it was right to boot him out of the world like this. Absurd to be so helpless! Ridiculous to be so absurd! Nevertheless, the ritual of derision did not fail him, secured his passage and kept him company all the way.

SONS ET LUMIÈRES

Even in the first instant of its fiat, the voice of God seemed badly dubbed, the words a curb in the mouth that outran sound. Nevertheless, at the end of time as at its beginning, cracked, clouded, flickering, thin, the light that responded touched everything with its original clarity, its first glory.

THE GIFT OF LIFE

In memory of Lionel Trilling

The age's principled ingratitude,
a viscous cant of self-begetting,
as if we *realized, fulfilled* a *self,*
who are indeed fictive and empty,
transparencies where eyebeams cross:
the points of intersection blaze
into sight, a sudden glory, light
looks back at light, star sees star,
and together are the shining of heaven.
And now and now and now an eye blinks off.

Unseen, I feel invisible, destroyed.
And every eye will shut away the luster,
and we and all will be again
the volatile nothing, and clear clear dark.

NEW POEMS

TO ALBERT COOK AND AARON ROSEN

THE THOUSAND NIGHTS AND
THE ONE NIGHT

King Shahryar was a dream of omnipotence distracted into bloody existence by his wife's infidelity.

Abandoned by maternal night, her faithfulness in which, innocent and whole, he'd slept, finding himself mortal, he became lethal, and each morning ordered time destroyed, whatever womb carried his seed—until Shahrazade, charming him with the spectacle of his helplessness, of a world he couldn't command, made him into a story and shut him up tight between the covers of a book.

Suspended in the mothering flow of her voice and jostled by the friendly turbulence of its flux of destinies, hearing himself told and retold, at one with his dreamer, King Shahryar sleeps happily.

And blue banners unfurling are all his days.

THE ECSTASIES

che fè Nettuno ammirar l'ombra d'Argo.
—DANTE

He swam, but swam in place, the place was his,
the whole of it, all the sea, and he its self
and sway, storming or still—and never still,
ecstatic platitude of the sea dazzle
and reaches, the dark reverie downward,
dreaming itself toward a fluent point
dispersed in a thousand silvery centers,
bubbles lofting and kissing themselves
into nothingness, the spray lifted and blown,
expatiating in broken syllables
—and he held close by the dream of the sea,
a wonder of water where he moved and touched
the light, saw the transparency, always
light moving, the clear ecstasy.
And splashed but couldn't speak, having no words
in the imageless sea. Then startled, started.
The little blindness of the marvelous
Argo's opacity pierced Neptune's brow,
and wavered into sound—the image sang,
and sang inside his coursing bones the in-
conceivable commonplaces, Sky, fire, star,
and offered him to all the openness.

THREE TALES

To Sanford Friedman

Why is there something and not nothing?
Because we have been spared.

CREATION

Out of himself matter and shining.
And now she smiles and swells.
Sky is mother, clear and cheering.
Sea is mother, strewn face upward

to heaven—blue, pellucid, fragrant,
a petal. She is pleased, she is pleasure,
gathering his light together.
On the seventh day I opened my eyes
and was good: looking, I lit;
seen, I shined—a spark
in space, space in a spark,
world in a world of worlds.
He lets the worlds go and goes away:

father hides in clarity
—how clear the endless seventh day!—
everywhere at rest, at play, calling: Children,
knock on my door!—But no one answered,
no one was there, the house was empty,
all of it open and ours entirely.
Teasing, he said: Look, here I am, I'm here!
We couldn't find him in the clarity,
and where we looked window, wall, and door
all were namelessly bright, all
were water, sky, and shore.
We flamed and flew in the ecstasy.

OGRES

(from an old manuscript)

. . . The land is his, his hunger the law.
What he gets he eats. I cannot endure . . .
Blood in the streets, the very streams
seem butchered, the sky a piece of meat . . .
A *friendly* horror (the mouth emits
a smile, the eyes just *show* their teeth)
takes them in hand, terrified, sick.
Armies of tots flogged toward his maw . . .
the nimble, the quick, the tender, the sweet . . .
gibberish of shrieks, then drivel of limbs.
I *saw* this, hidden in a heap of knuckles.
The little hands were still reaching . . .
I'm smeared with it. I feel nothing . . .

Later on I heard him explaining
(I scratch these words with splintered bone),
"Because, after all, I'm your father.
What else do you think I made you for?
You owe me everything, your food, your drink,
your being, the ruddy flesh off your backs . . ."
This was no figure of speech . . .
And then, "Ungrateful, where are you hiding?"
(The shark, too, complains of his prey,
Why aren't they more *forthcoming?*) . . .
Still later he was at his bookkeeping,
counting off on his fingers, muttering,
"Six days to get, fetter, fatten—that's
six days of fasting. On the seventh day
I eat." The monster! . . . *Moloch! Fiend!*
Leads each moppet up to the dish
and pointing all around he whispers,
"This is the world. You will die. Sorry, nipper."
. . . I caught him afterward asleep.
Still slobbering gore. Nothing fancy: I shoved
his jaw down his throat, sent the head flying . . .
This feeling of freedom, this joy . . .
Strange, for all the absence of ogres,
existence has proven no less fatal . . .
and every death marked Final.
The sky is gone, just swallowed up . . .
I think I'm dead, too. Look at him,
his chine stripped, his jaws still clacking . . .
I coolly fought to save my life . . .
no longer rage to keep my innocence.
I know who is my father's son.
Look at how they look at me,
push close with hunger, or run in horror.
Can't a man eat in peace anymore!
My kids still think they'll live forever.
I don't have immortality in my guts,
only a clot of frozen terror.
I'm hungry, too.
I'll poke down deep in theirs.
If there's any heaven in numbles,

I'll find it, I'll eat it all.
I'll teach them! *I'll* stop their staring . . .

SABBATH

Whose children are these advancing in me
to greet the little boat bearing the wide bliss
and lead it lamblike ashore by its painter?
Mouths, limbs bathed in a clarity not theirs,
where have I known them all before if not here,
pushing and dragging the sabbath dawn
up the beach with shouts and laughter,
scrambling for places and rowing the air?
There *was* no other world, *is* no other day!
Where are these flowers rushing in place
all the sunny afternoon?
The perfect speed of the daffodil
is the daffodil perfectly still.
Who are they, overturning it with dusk
and crawling under the hull to sleep,
lustrous voices, selves invisible?
Whom are they begging for stories now?
I *know* a story, it is their own:
These children have been, they will be, spared!
—Of all the worlds I made, this world alone
I did not destroy, but died instead.
Who am I, clear and dark over the sea,
dark and clear above the stars, the open
embrace, at once the greeting and goodbye?
Who will tell me while I understand?
What are they whispering snug all night
under the lulling rain, little and great?
Patter and pleasure of their sleepy conversing.
They name me *sacrifice*—their old man
is snoring; call me *sabbath* and *ending*
—the death consumed in clarity
—the clarity that makes the birth clear;
call me *distance*—and I depart;
the universe—I disappear
and am immortal and forget.

FAMILY HISTORY

GENEALOGY

My family tree is mist and darkness.
Century after century,
one lay upon the other begetting me.
Then my millennium in marshes
and wandering obscurity
revealed my heritage:
monster, I lack immortality,
my race is superfluous on earth.
The last, the final generation
—after me no other, or someone else—
I lay down on top of death.
We keep our appointments with fate,
even if fate does not;
though no one came to kill me, I died.
I the ghost that I begot.
My tree is night and fog.

MIT DEM SHPITS TSUNG AROYS*

The pink clue of mama's tongue,
the tip of it between her lips
when she concentrates, picking
at knots or threading a needle.
So she must have sat as a child,
a bit of sewing in her lap,
the tip of her tongue out showing
in imitation of her mother
or mother's mother—but I cannot
follow the clue any farther
and have nothing else to follow
into the lost domestic dark
of some small corner of the Pale.
Now she is patient but quick:
no false move, no motion wasted,

*Yiddish: with the tip of the tongue out.

nothing that needs doing over,
nothing overdone or stinted,
everything measured *so,*
sized up by eye and no
anxiety, no pedantry.
Only now have I understood
I have no better measure for
the fitness of things than her gesture,
dreamy and alert and left-handed,
of pulling a thread to length
while the spool runs 'round in her hand.
She is proud of herself as a worker,
tireless, versatile, strong,
both craftsman and laborer.
When she aims her thread at the needle,
her wide gray eyes intensify
—in them no want, no waste, no withering—
and it pleases her to say,
"Arbet macht dem leben ziess." *
Oh if it does, if it did
—though smeared in iron on the gate to hell—
then of hers the overflowing sweetness,
like a sugar tit touched to battered lips,
has made something of the darkness sweet.

IN THE EYE OF THE NEEDLE

Up on chairs as if they were floating
toward the kitchen ceiling, two sisters
are having hems set to the season's height,
to the middle of the knee, and no higher,
though they beg for half an inch, a quarter.
Robust and red-haired, they are two angels
beaming and grinning so they could never blow
the marvelous clarions their cheeks imply
—and I, fang still tender, venom milky,
small serpent smitten, witless with pleasure,
idling, moving my length along, spying,

* "Work makes life sweet."

summoned to Paradise by giggling
and chatter.
                    I saw this all
in the needle's eye—before time put it out—
compressed to two girls' gazes, hazel-eyed
and blue-eyed, one gentle, one imperious,
the soul at focus in its instant of sight,
expressive, shining there, revealed;
the seed of light flew down, a spark, two bits
of human seeing, and lay upon my heap
of gazes, bliss inexhaustibly blazing.

THE SINGER'S SINGER

"Vos zol ton a Yid? Epes a shneider." *

David at his harp, humming and clanking.
Fifty years of this have rounded his back,
and bending forward *looks* like prayer.
His rocking feet speed the iron treadle,
the needle fangs down faster and faster,
under the little foot, little teeth,
rising up, feed the cloth forward, male
and female together. Allegories
everywhere! A holy era for sure!
With rags, with crazy remnants he saved
—hoods and motley and mops and stars—
he pieces a garment together, cut
to no pattern, sizeless, mad, its unity
a oneness of confusion. "Old fool,"
I say, "what living man would wear your suit?
You sew for monsters, or sew for no one."
He glances up, blue eyes still squinting:
"The stone wall of terror on which you break
your head: nothing can be thought, nothing
can be done—and so, to do something,
to think nothing, you break your head.
You don't break down. You won't break through.
I, too. I sew an endless suit

*Yiddish: "What should a Jew do? [Shrugging.] A tailor."

to clothe the mist and keep it warm
and give it any shape I can.
My son, my son, here, please put it on."

CLOUD OF BRIGHTNESS

Who stood in cloud and made it shine?
Stupidity, confusion—in these, yes—
then faltering, refusal, feigning,
hiding in these, I returned
toward your presence, cheeks burning,
bold eyes aflame in the hooded places
—yes, I denied you in these.
I would not go forward,
swerved, balked, evaded;
at every forking chose
the farther way, savoring
everything I put, in secret, between
—the world my mask, my teasing.
And where you stood, distant, the cloud
thickened and glowed up brighter.
No matter, I would go away farther.
A world off still, I stood
before you, guilty, contrite
(these, too, disguises), and dared not
look away and dared not see
the being, brightness in the cloud.
Nonetheless, in his sanctuary
of punishment a child dares everything.
I greeted blindness, terror
of total dark, the cloud of myself
—only so, malingerer
in midst of glory, can I
recover my good will
from black mineral.
I cannot spy who sees me,

shut eyes or look aside.
I am seen completely.
So must I wish to be seen,
since law is: of you can we know
in measure as we are revealed.
No other darkness intervenes,
no light bright enough to see.
I know your bashfulness.
Shine now to the blind
your shy epiphany.

ROWING ON THE ACHERON

These two sitting across a table
suddenly were seated side by side
out rowing on the Acheron.
She'd asked, "How often have you died?"

Could one embrace so close to hell,
he might have caught her emptiness
against his empty breast and made,
perhaps, a shade or two the less.

"How often have you *failed* to die?"
He mocked at her? and with his pain?
The prisoner of dialectics
can never cease rattling his chain.

So, two moving solitudes—so oar
and oar to either side—kept pace
on a stream so small, so shallow
they might have left it any place.

It seemed now not to matter if
the immortality in reach,
the universe aching to speak,
should never choose them for its speech.

The river they rode on moved in them.
She craved its flowing identities,
he to pass beyond remembering.
Failure, too, has voluptuaries.

Each saw as each was: she, on her side,
a savior take her death and die;
on his, Pluto, scavenging for lives,
was tossing back the lesser fry.

Her vivid bones a jetting flame;
he a crystal nothing could consume.
But here came the waiter with the check,
the busboy sweeping past with a broom.

Delicate, swift, their waking glance
exchanged the vision each had seen,
their next was blank, the last returned
their smiles, and set the table between.

MAN OF LETTERS

All that was not Napoleon was a little corner,
a book half open, where L. labored unceasingly.
He called it his very own, himself.

And because Napoleon's name was loudly
everywhere, an offense and distraction to L.,
a bare bulb blazed in obliteration there
that never shadow come or his creep out.
Barren light, bare place made show of virtue.

An enemy of shadow *and* a friend to light?

L. elbowed around a mousetrap in mock couvade:
and whenever rumor of Napoleon encroached,

like a loser at cards L. would be muttering,
"Biography, biography, enough
biography, just stick to the text!"

—as he had stuck, concentrating so fiercely
the mousetrap bristled an indignant perfection:
too good for mere mice, repellent to the world
it should compel—unless, he wished, there is one
worthier than this supine, this besotted world.

Such dilemmas allow one solution.

The mousetrap works to perfection—little
by little it has taken (he has given) all his life.

And who can better make a mousetrap than a mouse?

It looks, deceptively, like a tongue-in-cheek.

"Napoleon, don't you believe it, I mean business!"

O foolish little L., misled by envy
to make himself a rival to his enemy,
by ambition to covet the Lion's share!

Is it the world he hears? And Napoleon
bounding after? Surely, someone is out there
clawing and caterwauling in ecstasy,
thumping the earth beyond the doorway,
demanding to consume his whole production!

Success is being wooed by an avalanche.

Too late, too late! A time bomb ticking too quickly,
already his breathless squeaks cry back,
"Coming, coming, sir, I'll unlatch in one second,
no worry, plenty here for everyone,
special L-shaped beauty just for you,
expertly crafted, ready to snap,
bam! like so, word will swallow world,

all life in a text, your last meow, sir,
if I can be your author, creep into my corner,
you must be little before you can be greater,
time to shut the book—scrouch down, more, more, more,
advance your dear paw now a tiny bit farther . . .

And fable and fame and world and cat
and light and L. and all are one, are not.

THE HUMAN CIRCLE

At a *vernissage* and then next day again
at the poetry reading—the same faces.
No, other faces had undergone a like
refiguration, a leveling estrangement:
Picasso persons, each with paired visages
(and a third queasily both and neither),
a crowd of aunts, uncles, cousins by aging,
as if a common gene of caricature
was unmasking itself in them; and yet
their furious tippling and chatter before
the gilded driftwood on the walls—chilling with
the tomb's disparagement of speech—or mutual
hailings next day while I shuffled my pages
did not persuade me their recognitions
were welcome, their reunions joyful.
Gaunt or puckered, with tanned-over wrinkles,
hair thinned to floating white wisps, enfeebled
—oh I knew they all were strangers, yet seemed
deformed familiars from another world
or perfections there degraded in this,
say, lords and ladies of Byzantium
gone to ground one summer in South- and East Hampton.
They, of course, were looking back with glances
saying they almost remembered my feather
—whatever kind of bird I thought myself—

their puzzling eyes all but squinted the words
What, you, too? How you have changed—nephew!
It's true, I was the youngest there of all the old.

I remember that I sat waiting, to one side
on a metal chair, in the state of someone
about to perform, intense, and removed farther
by intensity, not nervous, but like
a racehorse in the gate: I was mad to go
—without knowing where to or what I'd say
or whether hired to please or to harrow,
or entertain or prophesy or confess
—or all of these, and out of my entrails,
inoffensively of course, charmingly
if I could, with a slight bending of the neck,
a certain exposure of the throat.
Or knew to whom I was to read my stuff,
or what they wanted, coming as they did
—as I supposed—week after week all summer long
to hear unremarkable actors, in ordinary
clothes, without sets or music, and poorly lit,
intone their mostly lackluster scenarios.
Perhaps I'd been invited to tarnish quietly
for an hour—in the dampish basement of
a dreadful cult of mediocrity.
They knew me? Bards of a feather? Welcome, *nephew!*
Well, and who *did* I think I was writing for?
Beautiful illiterates wholly alive?
Too arrogant to look down, abashed
to raise my eyes, I stared straight ahead—then stood,
hearing myself introduced. Nobody,
at least, was chewing gum or taking notes.

And they all fell silent,
as the dead do,
who lock themselves away
and not for anything
will ever come out.
The silence of the dead
is a lifetime's silences,

speech subtracted and withheld
from the living circle,
a sum of immortality
stored up in powerful jaws.
Therefore, the stories of the dead
are also the living speech
of the human circle.

Once there was a little village—so went the story I told—once
there was a little village, a human circle that filled its world
completely.

From nowhere, a stranger came, stateless, exile or wanderer.
Of him, they knew, they could know, nothing—he was
entirely a secret, was secrecy become visible, seeming, in
silence, to stand closer to each than any did in speaking.

Now they perceived *their* secrecy, the unstated power each held
against every other—not particular, paltry secrets but a
powerful will to secrecy, in which all shared: a shadow and
substitute village, not the human circle but its opposite and
enemy.

He understood, darkly, that it was given to him to reveal the
story and renew the circle; so *he* would stand revealed, be
reinstated.

Someone dies; he, too, dresses in death, puts on the pelt of
silence, the dog's head and paws, and, feigning death, lies
down beside the dead one. With furtive claws he tears at
the hypocritical death, he drives his muzzle into it. Now he
woos the dead one with silence more powerful than the
silence of death, singing, *I know you live, and will lead you
back to the place of the living. Arise, and come forth!* Snatches
its silence and runs. A glance—the bones fall back.

In his mouth the secret is raging as if, possessed, it were his
secret. He speaks it, but out of nowhere it howls aloud to
the human circle: *I am alive! I live!*

Its cry is the power coursing from each to each.

It roars in the applause rising against the silence to celebrate
the immortal covenant of the living. And welcomes back
the scavenger.

"We are alive!" they all cried out.

Noises roused me from the story I was telling
the dying. Not fifty yards away,
higher than our heads, invisible
in the chill summer fog, Atlantic combers
were booming through the late afternoon.
Apparently, I had been reborn here,
in a museum cellar, where some new power
announced itself in their quickening hands:
they were applauding themselves with full hearts,
me with faltering confidence
—I could see their mouths and eyes,
the good humor of one, in the other
the horror.
                    But each at last to his own house.
So, the circle broke, each one
not less secretive but going
with his secret lightly,
like readers of stories who, silent themselves,
are revealed to the world of revelation
—while I remained a moment among the chairs,
grinning, and bowing my head.

ELEGIES

FIRST

As the life goes on it starts to double
and loop over; acquaintances, chance meetings,
poems, places recur tumbling in the backflow,
grinding together to indifferent likeness
or pounded bare of old senses but senselessly
inscrutable now: what *could* they have been?
were they ever themselves and not their substitutes?
were we ourselves and not our make believe?
did we touch then and speak, touch as we spoke?
And our stories were truer for touching?

our contact more generous for our phrases,
the human circle larger, more hospitable?
That is past mentioning, past believing,
bubble now, or gravel clattering.
And others move in our manner, speak our mouthings?
This mimicry doesn't flatter,
mockery where not a curse
—a stale folly feeds a fresh disgust.
Time palpable and conscious in us.
Not ourselves; said nothing; these things never were;
muddle of grit and figments:

       the juvenile
poet, death's blabbing messenger boy
in one elegy I wrote, four years later
was the message other couriers spoke;
the young Spaniard to whom I translated "X,"
in three weeks himself a dead child
—indentured both to the same bully;
this poem, begun before a death, may yet
endure to include others: I feel at times
I am writing in a race with horror
—dregs of anecdote I can bear no longer,
smoothing in my swell, in meditation;
I will crash, and course at random,
myself confounded in myself;
can the breaker say what
is what? tell what from what?
I drink my drowning.
Shameful if one takes the bully's part.
Your corpse, now, is your true impostor.
And each of us comes lugging one home,
a griping in the wave's bowel.
Grief or grievance? mourning or self-pity?
A thousand-mouthed turbulence is roaring
for eternity.

    Time breaks the bubbles of stone,
drowns the sparks in the cunning baubles.
I have kept nothing entire, clear, alive,
having broken my words, quenched my vow
—how will I authorize reality?

Seeing these things, one sees
one has lived too long, outlived too many.
Pastiche of being, duplicitous, demeaning.
Your impostor is your posterity.
Some other is seizing my I, my speech. I repeat myself.
I am myself repeated.
The surf's tooth snags on sand, worries, gnawing
one spot, roars; it will go no farther;
too ample to be intelligible,
the thunderous echo engulfs the glittering original,
yet is powerless to tell the story, move these words upward.

SECOND

We wake to poetry from a deeper dream,
a purer meditation—expanse of light
in water pressing unquenched on our eyes;
we swam in seeing, our bodies saw. . . .
Voices distracted me and I awoke
. . . and after the voices died remain
wakeful at midnight near children,
telling them stories, what the voices spoke.
Our tales evoke a living circle,
chime among presences, possess the sound
of being heard; we hear them so, resonant
with listeners, who come close in the dark;
our tales are such late echoes of loss,
but a promise of recovery,
the deeper dream come back as the common place.
And so we shape our stories to acknowledge
company present, include them, name
and feature, in the tale, narrow to their span
the girth of powers telling calls up out
of the turbulent nothing—and they rouse,
they come ashore glistening, plunge
toward being, while their riders, swift
in the stillness of the tale, crouch
whispering into the ears of the dark
—it is darkness the children are riding,
our words in their newborn voices

rich nonsense free of our perplexity,
our rage, of living, too trivial,
too precious to mean anything ever,
and the darkness listens as it runs—
Yes, go, *Beauty! Wind! Time!*

I am those words
alive in their mouths
while they speak me;
I am their breath,
the missing companion
who comes again
and again to the lips;
and air that lives
in their telling;
the evocation alive
in the air.
And laugh to live on,
so pure and senseless
a spell
      —if only I
do not survive
my posterity.

How quick the horses ran,
how quiet under the earth.
Was it a waking dream?
inside a dream of sleep?
They rode and whispered too well.
I have been telling to the air
this story the children will never tell.

THIRD

Voices roused him and he woke.
Or say he stumbled into wakefulness, found himself on all fours
    peering over a doorsill. In the dark, bignesses—bulk or
    shadow—blocked his way to the light and out.
And say they rumbled and hissed in every part and movement,
    and this was their speech, outlandish gabble that made *him*

the stranger, not the denizen he'd thought. And that they hid nothing meant he was no guest either, but someone extra, of no account, in fact, no one at all.

Say their number was indeterminate: two, or several, many more, one; in every form dangerous. So he called all the same: bully—and kept his vigil.

Say, latecomer, squatter, bully could dispose of him as bully wished; his being here, his very existence were scurf, the skin of nothingness. Cleverness might keep him alive (bully was strong, bully was dumb), it could do nothing to clarify his status, or the status of anything. He crouched down better.

Say he might hope someday to become mascot to a team of gods. Forget it! Or say benevolent despot—and show bully how bully ought to be. Fat chance!

Say, seeing little, he heard much, overheard, rather, since bully addressed only itself or muttered back and forth to themselves. Just as well; he would not have believed anything bully said to him directly. Always with an ear out while seemingly dawdling, hanging around; always on the ball of one foot pivoting, veering with the voices—no blast of bully's might catch him broadside; at last, little more than an ear, overgrown, overhearing.

Say bully was unworthy of such delicacy; he was too considerate, really, he should have torn the words from bully's throat.

Say the voices turned for worse—the rude banter louder, the hissing ominous. Most miserably: in his fear he had nothing to cling to but the very thing he feared. So he hung there by his ear, hearing.

Say this moment of his conception filled his ear to overflowing; now he conceived of himself: he was the other, the third person of bully's discourse, the *he,* as it were, of bully's brutish hee-hawing.

Say outrageous to discuss him *in absentia;* still, he dared not by any peep signify his presence; discovered, he would be hurled down and made to vanish, the subject of a sentencing he would never hear or know ever was being carried out. Thus, unassuageable his terror of absence.

Say, unable to bear more, he made of the murderous din a phrase to mumble over and over, rocking himself in his arms where he crouched and crooned to his failing heart.

Say it saved him—this sentence of death that became his charm, his talisman, the anthem of his being and secret motto of self-denomination.

Say, long after, he understood all that racket, this *bully bully bully* he was forever mumbling; in that moment, also, he forgot it; and, forgetting, uttered it as his own. Now he was in the other room, his shadow longer, solid. Amnesia would do as innocence. He suspected nothing. He had arrived.

Say a small figure, a mere curlicue of being—himself or another—crouches at the doorsill, peering over.

Say this story he overhears him telling.

FOURTH

Three selves of me set out together.
Stooped and strident, I did worship power
and take the bully's part—the side of death—
against me, stooped, defiant: I cast me out
and left me there to die raging among stones.
Two of me went on together. At Three Roads,
I rose up and, striking back, struck me down.
Stooped and white now, I, the third of three,
surviving both, fare onward alone,
telling my bloody story with one hand out.
That is all I know how: suffer, sup, survive,
perform for the world world's scandal of self
—See *me!* clamor I, squeal out, Why *me?*
if pinch squeeze in, yet quick, given
the respite of a single breath, to wink
and sneak a grab for crust or crotch.
In secret, I am proud—whoever
this I is, who, surrounded by death
on every side, crows here and now.

FIFTH

To move forward with the world, to be
in time with time . . . is innocence.
For a thousand miles the wave keeps pace,

strokes smoothly on in phase with force,
at one with the festive crowd
and one of its joyous more and more;
it buoys itself and drives ahead,
renews in the trough the power it
expends at the crest, shape it then
surpasses and leaves to lapse behind.
I love my innocence, it chants,
see my transparence, I have nothing to hide,
therefore, I cannot ever die;
my existence is benign, the air
I breathe is borrowed from no one;
the drowning see my breath and smile
—except the evil, whose badness starves them,
monsters, they merit their bulging eyes.
I bask and sing, am smooth and shine.

The figure in the wave, kneeling, half dazed,
half drowned, battering its head on the ground,
lifted and pushed forward inches, chokes
and blusters into the water running down. . . .
Out of time, sea-sick, sucking
the slack scum between wave and wave, here
is what you discover in the reflux:
the theme of age, the falsity of innocence
—your every breath an act of power,
you live to injure, survive by murder;
while you were lethal, you were innocent;
floundering in the raging slop,
powerless now, you grasp the fact of power.
Your lung half bitter broth, you blurt:
Existence is my enemy, my life
attacks me; my past, maimed and vengeful,
returns in a wave, is heaving inside me;
my retching rises to possess me—the dead,
large with my past power, overpower me.
Grievance is death usurping my throat,
is death already speaking out as me.
—And you struggle to spit it all out,

you struggle not to go under, struggle
to assent to indeed go under as
an equal who negotiates with death.

SIXTH

I want to tell my story to the ground
I want to whisper my trouble to the earth
I want to lie down and ease my heart
I want to put my mouth to the ear of earth
I want to fill my mouth with dirt
I want to fill my eyes with darkness
—let earth be my sight! the fallen earth
poor old lady earth, poor queen, poor body
I want to feel each grain against me
I want to be clay and marry with clay
Let my words be stifled! there is no story
it has all been told, I have nothing to say
I want to unloose and subside, and seep away
I want to follow the sparks below gravity
I want to quench my glory, shining offends me
I want to be November in the clay
The cold slime will not frighten me
I want to vanish, why should I stay
—exile is my homeland
I want to know nothing I want to see nothing
say nothing be nothing never again
I want to tell my sorrow to the ground

SEVENTH

On the hill's top, hidden by rocks,
they nuzzle its tender sleep
—the infant is found.

Out of flame, half goat himself—shank of goat
and scrotum—the goatboy scrambles and mounts,
driving his clattering nannies ahead.
Humps over the hill, the steep stone.

205

What soft flame spurts from his reed?
What light step in the last pasture?

Messenger, thief, smuggler of souls,
middleman between two worlds, rattling
two dice in his hand, he dodges and runs
among the brush and boulders halfway up.
Death is stupid, though strong,
outwitted at every instant but one.
His craft and laughter break the boundaries,
confound the bad faith of too much talk,
the target's self-pitying palaver
—the higher the art, the greater the imposture,
the more complete the metamorphoses.
Leaping from the glitter on the sea,
the rays in flight are a clashing of knives.
He trusts his luck—the world's complicity
in his existence—takes refuge in a risk,
in randomness, ducks and dodges:
around, the blazing moments flash and miss,
flashing past, sting the stone fell of death;
his darting dazzles—quicksilver itself,
he catches light and flings it far;
rays light harmlessly everywhere
—in the moment he is immortal!
and gone in a flash—the blaze
    of his evasions, his blazing visions
are one.

Mutter tap mutter cough shuffle spit
On the lowest slope, the old tragedian,
stooped under his load of solemnity
and pathos, his satchel of used soliloquies,
creeps upward in the foul cleft
of a garbage-clogged ravine.
Mutter tap mutter cough shuffle spit
And carries two small harbor stones, twin eggs
from the sea, to bury on the hill's high
summit of rubble over his own bald brow.

EIGHTH

Death is mindless, like gossip
—these dregs of anecdote we cast
hopefully at our glass houses,
or cast toward one another simply
to be rid of, passing on what
can't be thought, what bears only
the interest of iteration,
fool's gold, chunks of pugnacious fact,
or fiction stupefied as fact.
Fools, of course, we are avid for them,
as hens are for hard baubles
with which to grind the daily fare.
So our dead return to figure in
the stories we tell—not to remain
unthinkable, not to be cast off
as odd, inert, mere facts of matter.
And that they keep returning is
the tale that clearly becomes them,
the one that keeps us at our telling,
keeps us gossiping across the grave
about every imaginable thing.
They are emissaries to absence,
who bear our tales beyond our voices,
and speak for us—of us—to all the dead
in their past and vanished country,
repeating our tales of sun and cloud,
what we murmur into their eternal blink
to tell them how it is today with light,
with dark, such weathers of consciousness
as we, moment by moment, wander in.
And they return with news of nothingness,
their quietness of someone listening,
in which, finally, we hear ourselves
speaking and heard, absent and here,
in passage and lingering as we step off,
ourselves and other—these revenants
who press to our own their missing faces.

Without this, we would—when all is told—
be poor indeed in a well-lit dead end,
the bright misery of a shadeless world.

EVER AFTER

To Noemi

The beginning was all a puzzlement:
the small mouth in the sand, its dark trickle,
pain she wanted to run from and couldn't,
then a fiery thistle of fingers
pointed or waggled or beckoned or prodded
or said Pay attention! Her eyes, bright-new,
were coin for that: she kept still and looked
—however hard to know what was a sign
or just a self idling beside the road
and did it mean her, whoever she was.
Still, she went on, getting the knack of it,
and little by large everything opened up,
the signs leading onward to other signs,
the riddles rearing in her path like stiles,
too high to jump but easy to slip under;
and misplaced whatever had to be found
again, and followed every misdirection
until it came true, and ran needless errands
so whatever else had to happen could,
so the white horse who came to her in the wood
would come to her saddled and carrying
a king, and believed unbelievable witches
and little wizards her body sensed were kin,
and by subtle experiment and profound
meditation discovered her powers
and the power of her prince-making kiss,
too extraordinary almost to use.
And so it was so, after all—and all
that often-diverting foolery had led

somehow to a state figured in the stars:
every night she saw a kingdom go to sleep,
and, gleaming shoe buckle to sparkling
diadem, rose and possessed the heavens.

And saw, from the height of her life, she had lived
a story, had, as though enchanted, obeyed
the dumb talk gesturing in her limbs, while she
—her passionate hunger for mysteries
nothing that merely happened could sate—
had wagered herself against everything,
demanding always, "And now? What happens now?"
And now? And now she was telling the story,
an old woman talking to children.
Words came to her, so perfectly at the pace
of things they seemed not to move at all—and now
the odd details of her journey grew lucid,
the wilderness, at home in itself, made sense.
And telling it again made the same sense
again, made it deeper, gave it pleasure,
the water came up in the bucket clearer,
from a cooler, stiller depth of the well,
and where the bucket knocked the wellcurb
the wood buffed itself clean on the stone,
until her life lay clear in the grain.
She touched it, beautiful, neutral, itself.
"Ever after" was really the afterlife
where she would be telling her life over.
No longer checked, exhorted, driven
in an agony of forwardness,
the fierce horse walks over the tranquil plain,
bobbing its nose in an oaken pail.
The children reach down to pat its flanks.
She is happy. So.
                    And once again
let herself drop until no bigger than
a pale thimble in the deep, but bountiful
and great when she brought the darkness up
on her lips, potable and clear and filling,
and touched them so to the children's lips;

and, gleaming shoe buckle to sparkling
diadem, rose and by all ways at once
kicked free and scattered across the heavens.

THE TORTOISE

Surely he deemed himself swiftness personified, muttering as
he went, My name is Diligence, I am Alacrity: I leap to serve.
Yet while one or another blazing messenger came and left a
thousand times, the tortoise on the vestibule floor—at each
flitting shadow, at the trembling of flagstones under the
skimming feet, at the little buffets of air—paused a thousand
times to rehearse his ancient repertoire of discretions. As if all
this coming and going were aimed against him, or against the
word he bore most carefully within.

Comic or pathetic he may seem to those of us who measure
his miles as inches, who at every stride hurdle a hundred
diapasons—yet the throne room shall greet the tortoise with
unstinted glory and the new message entrusted him shall be no
less urgent, no less momentous.

Then see the majesty of his slow turning, his smile of wis-
dom too wise to smile, see how high his foot is lifted!